T0117048

GERRY BURKE

PEST TAKES A CHANCE

... and Other Humorous Stories from the Paddy Pest Chronicles

Pest Takes a Chance
... and Other Humorous Stories from the Paddy Pest Chronicles

iUniverse books may be ordered through booksellers or by contacting:

iUniverse
1663 Liberty Drive
Bloomington, IN 47403
www.iuniverse.com
844-349-9409

ISBN: 978-1-4620-1444-6 (sc)
ISBN: 978-1-4620-1445-3 (hc)
ISBN: 978-1-4620-1443-9 (e)

Print information available on the last page.

iUniverse rev. date: 12/11/2020

EXPLANATORY NOTES

David Walkden is a friend of mine who first raised the possibility that I could have an alter ego who was both successful and incompetent within the intelligence community. I treated his suggestion with scant respect until I realized that Inspector Clouseau, Maxwell Smart and Johnny English had already dipped their toe in this gene pool. So was born Patrick Pesticide, aka Paddy Pest.

Due to the fact that Mr Pest is likely to get a swelled head should I give him total control of this book, I have restricted his adventure stories to a manageable number. I believe that my readers will be grateful for small mercies.

ACKNOWLEDGMENTS

Editing Services: Kylie Moreland

INTRODUCTION

For some time now, I have been providing opinion and social commentary on subjects that are close to my heart: politics, entertainment, sport and travel. I even have my own brand name, PEST.

This moniker has something to do with the fact that most folks flee through the nearest exit when they see me coming. Nevertheless, these people are very dear to me and I have decided to tell some of their stories in a way that is only marginally litigious. Some of the names have been changed to protect the innocent.

My indefatigable crime fighter, Paddy Pest, is a long way from being innocent. He likes to tell his own stories and so I have let him loose, knowing full well that he is likely to shock and offend, more often than not. It is probably his Irish background.

Sometimes, I get very cross with myself for intruding into my own personal experiences in order to entertain my readers but I am sure that you are worth it. I certainly hope that you didn't buy this book just because it was cheap.

Gerry Burke

TABLE OF CONTENTS

–1–

THE PADDY PEST CHRONICLES

Paddy Pest is a fictional character who reminds me very much of myself: sometimes charming but mostly abrupt, impertinent and totally frustrating. He travels the world on a loose arrangement with certain intelligence agencies that continue to deny any association with him or his equally vile cronies. As an undercover agent and crime fighter, he spends an inordinate amount of time under the covers. In fact, the less said about his sleeping arrangements the better.

I suppose that he will worm himself into your affections as he takes you on his ridiculous adventures. Quite frankly, I wouldn't believe a word of it.

PEST IN A PICKLE

I always seem to be able to get myself into a jam, but in all honesty, I don't know how I managed to get myself locked up in the storeroom of the Acme Preservation Company. The factory was situated in the industrial part of town, not a good place to be when the sun goes down. I had received a tip-off that something bad was going down and I needed to be there. I'm not sure why. The source of the information had come from a dame who had the best tips in the business.

Stormy Weathers was a lady of indeterminable age, who was mine host at a disreputable night-club in a rather seedy part of the city. I was one of their regular disreputable customers. The intelligence service that occasionally utilized my services liked to employ colorful sleeper agents and Stormy was as radiant as a rainbow. Although the lady spent a lot of time in bed, she didn't do much sleeping. Her clientele were also quite colorful and might I say, a bit flashy. I should add that most customers were men because that's the kind of establishment it was, a gentlemen's club.

If you scan the employment records or annual reports of any national security agency, you won't find the name Paddy Pest listed. Just look for the page that identifies petty cash disbursements. The relevant sub-heading will be described as such:

Payments to whistle-blowers, stool-pigeons, narks, finks and other scum!

I will be in there somewhere, as inconspicuous as possible. The good thing is that I have a working brief to follow my nose and if the information I provide is tasty enough, the bread comes my way. However, as previously mentioned, I can sometimes get myself into a bit of a jam.

So it was that I found myself outside the pickle factory at midnight. Stormy Weathers had been privy to a private conversation between two rancid reprobates and felt obliged to pass on that information to yours truly. In this instance, it was easy to follow my nose. My arrival coincided with an onion delivery from one of the interstate market gardens. I thought that this was a strange time to make a delivery. The pickle factory was only a division of Acme Preservations and all the other factories on the site were closed and boarded up for the night.

Before I proceed any further with this tale, I know that there are questions that you will want to ask, including:

"Do you carry a gun?"

The short answer is "Yes, but not one particular firearm."

I like to co-ordinate my weapons with my attire. You can never hide a 44 Magnum under your clothes, so one often reverts to a Glock or a Heckler and Kock. For a while I was using a Walther PPK but once James Bond made them fashionable, they became a pricy item and hard to obtain. As it proved, I needed more artillery at the pickle factory. My sidearm was a small Beretta, which didn't give me the fire power that I needed. Who would have expected to be up against a rocket launcher?

The rocket launcher was in the van with the onions, a devilish good camouflage. I didn't know whether the terrorists had an immediate target in mind but it wasn't difficult to come to the conclusion that this factory was where they kept their arms cache. Later, it would be determined that Acme was a front for Allah's Corp of Militant Extremists.

As you might think, I was a little worried about what could happen to me should I be exposed but, then again, the kind of kudos and remuneration that I might expect from the agency made me salivate. I decided to consider my options and retired to a small ethnic café around the corner, where the proprietor carved off some mouth-watering lamb from the spit and served it up with salad and a spicy baba ganoush.

Some minutes later, the driver of the onion truck walked in and proceeded to barter with the owner. They were speaking in a language that was foreign to me but eventually it seemed a deal was made and two men returned with a few cases of onions. I used this diversion to slip into the night and then through the door of the factory. I don't like to be a spokesman for commercial interests but if you are ever keen to do a bit of slipping and sliding, I can thoroughly recommend Hush Puppies for your feet. That night, I was sneaking in and around packing cases on floors that were both shiny and rough and nary a squeak. In fact, I probably wouldn't have been discovered if I hadn't farted.

I managed to ditch the Beretta before they came at me and this was just as well. The thugs had no idea that I was any kind of investigator and probably assumed that I was a vagrant who was looking for some warm accommodation. This may have been due to the half bottle of cheap spirits that they found on my person.

"Hey, dumbdick! Don't you know this is an alcohol-free environment?"

"It's only for medicinal purposes," I stammered, in mock fear, as they searched through my intimate apparel and patted me down with rough hands. I could only be glad that it wasn't Stormy that they were groping. Certainly, she wouldn't take to Mr Onion-breath and his gruff approach.

They locked me in one of the storerooms until they could report to someone with higher authority. On the way to my prison, I glanced into a side room and saw camera equipment and a collection of hari-kari swords. I was glad that I hadn't made any plans for my forthcoming birthday.

The thing about beheading people is that it can be rather messy. Your blood vessels never get any kind of warning and so they have no time to formulate a managed exit strategy. Blood just spurts everywhere. I think that this is why they decided to dispose of me in a different way and I don't need to explain what happens when you are included as part of the pickle ingredients, crushed and stirred. By the time the finished product gets to the bottling plant, any extraneous bones and hard matter have been adequately pulverized and the slightly bitter taste is hardly discernable. Nevertheless, I expected that my taste would be very bitter. After all, that's exactly how I felt.

Back at Sam's Fly by Night Club, Stormy must have had some inclination that something was wrong. I don't believe that there was any particular reason for this way of thinking other than the fact that Paddy Pest invariably stuffs things up. She put in a call to Agency Central.

"I haven't heard from Paddy and Happy Hour is about to start. He would have to be in serious trouble to miss that."

The rescue team was soon sniffing around the factory perimeter. They would have smelled the same things that I did: onions. They may also have picked up on another aroma as I had shit myself in anticipation of my forthcoming execution. It is preferable to go to your death with some degree of dignity but when the time comes, even your insides try and escape.

The first inkling that escape was a possibility was when my captors dropped their hard line and offered me mortality alternatives. Naturally, I thought that I would be heading for the dill pickle vat but evidently there had been a delayed delivery of mangoes for the chutney and the herring quota was also a little short. I opted for the red herring as the fish tank was close to where I had hidden my Beretta. I figured that with my famous roll-over and rumble technique, I could take out two of them but the third terrorist would have the drop on me. I needn't have worried. The cavalry arrived just in time and Stormy put her eight inch dagger in between Hussein's ribs. Hussein was the hairy one and he fell into one of the vats and was well and truly pickled. We made it back to Sam's for the last ten minutes of Happy Hour.

Stormy Weathers: undercover agent

You may think that because I am more Maxwell Smart than James Bond, a hotty like Stormy Weathers would not be sweet on me but she was and her delight in being part of my rescue was quite apparent. In fact, her display of affection was most embarrassing to the other guys in the agency who were bound by ridiculous vows of morality and the like. They weren't even allowed to drink on the job.

The bean counters arrived and uncovered an arsenal of highly sophisticated military equipment and it was obvious that the bad guys had not been far away from a pre-emptive strike. Stormy and I were rewarded with the usual expressions of gratitude but this time, the agency dug deep for something more tangible: a two week layover in the Caribbean. And layover we did. The door to our bungalow wasn't opened for three days and then only to allow for room service and the restocking of the bar.

When we finally emerged, I concluded that it was good to be out and about. After all, this was the playground of Ian Fleming, Graham Greene, Noel Coward and the ruthless Dr No. We even made a booking for the *I Spy Club* before discovering that it was a hang-out for swingers and voyeurs. The British Embassy was just as you might expect, all walls and whitewash, just like me. Even Stormy commented that I cut a dashing figure in my white linen suit: the suit that she had picked out for me.

There were other eyes on me that day, the day I was refined and refitted by the lady that I loved. Of course, I hadn't told her that but I think she must have had an idea. After all, why else would she commit to helping me change my ways? Perhaps women just can't help themselves.

The inquisitive eyes were shaded by a straw hat with a large brim. In the shadow of a narrow lane way, a lazy wasp of tobacco smoke gave up the snoop as a cheroot smoker. This meant that he was probably not to be trusted. Usually, I would cover my back and be prepared for anything but because I was on holidays, I had become a little casual in maintaining my vigilance.

The snatch was perfectly coordinated and I have to admit that we contributed to the ease of the operation. Stormy had stopped in front of a street vendor and was haggling over the price of something. I was using the spare time to pop a few blackheads that were worrying me when a screech of car tires heralded an urgency that I had not previously noticed in the country before. The smell of burning rubber had hardly dissipated when I recognized a far more insidious aroma: chloroform.

I awoke in darkness and called out for Stormy. She was not there. A gull in the distance helped me with my bearings. I was still on this earth and near the sea. The word *panic* is not in my vocabulary but I have to admit that I have never liked the dark. I wondered if my abductors were informed and aware of this fact. The hours slipped by. There was no food or water provided and I had certainly missed that day's episode of Oprah. These were heartless people.

The grating noise of a sliding panel awoke me from my reverie.

"Good evening, 0027. I hope that you haven't been too uncomfortable."

Oh no! They had mistaken me for one of those goons from MI6. Who is the idiot in charge of their research – Huckleberry Finn? And no matter how much Mr Big speaks through that handkerchief, he is not going to disguise the fact that he was the chap we had dinner with the night before. He was as camp as a row of tents.

There were no demands made on that first night and, in fact, I was offered any number of items to make my stay more comfortable. In an effort to ingratiate myself with the woolly woof, I asked for fresh flowers and some Bette Midler music. As a compromise, he piped in the Village People for fourteen hours on end. I will never stay at the YMCA again.

Stormy was pretty upset that we had been duped so easily and I knew that she would be hot on the trail of the perpetrators of this brazen kidnap. The sad thing was that the British Embassy was reluctant to help. "Who is this chap, Paddy Pest? Is he an Australian?"

"Why don't you see Christopher Case? He comes from that neck of the woods."

Chris Case had been a high flyer in the days when all you needed was an idea and a bank overdraft. He had trains, planes, boats, women and twelve hours start when it all went pear shaped. For some reason, these kinds of people always gravitate to the sun. The roustabout lad from the Australian outback moved from one sunny paradise to another with sufficient funds to grease hands and ease the relocation blues. It appeared that he was to be my only chance of salvation.

For their first meeting, Stormy wanted to impress, so she wore a little red satin number with a slit up the side. I am told that he nearly gagged on his martini. I know what you are thinking. If he feels this way about her, he may actually be enthusiastic about my anticipated demise. Of course, people who think this way don't know much about Aussie blokes and how we will always go that extra mile for a mate in trouble. Nevertheless, he was drooling – not a good sign.

You may wonder why Stormy turned to Chris for help. The fact is that for the past few years, he had kept two steps ahead of his pursuers and always had his ear to the ground. The island was volcanic and underground caves were scattered all over the place. There was a good chance that I was in one of them.

"This must be very sad for you, my dear. I have had my ear to the ground and have heard nothing. Would you like another martini?"

Back in my dungeon, I was attempting a mental analysis of my tormentor. I guessed that he was a deranged psychopath rather than a calculating industrialist with a chip on his shoulder and a desire for world domination. These people are extremely dangerous and should be treated with contempt. I was worried that there was still no attempt at engaging with me on any level other than those animal things that my captor kept pushing under the door. Patrick Pesticide was brought up with death adders, red-back spiders and the like. Mom used to mash them on the breakfast griddle and mix in a pungent Vegemite sauce. Delicious!

In London, the villain had finally made contact and the executive team was called in for a late night meeting at MI6 headquarters. His demands were quite simple. In return for the safe release of agent 0027, the government was to pledge support for gay marriage in Britain and throughout the Commonwealth. It was a contemporary version of some film script that I had read. The real agent 0027 must have thought that this was a real giggle. He was presently enjoying some downtime on the French Riviera with a lady who had been married three times.

The first reaction from the powers that be was to treat this as some kind of a joke but somebody leaked the story to Rolf Harris and Dame Edna Everage and they went into bat for their fellow citizen.

"Rolfy, one of our boys is in trouble. Should we send Sir Les over to comfort poor Stormy?"

Sir Les Patterson was a man of embarrassing personal habits and he was sure to arrive at Government House with his fly undone. Instead, the Queen sent a message of support and Prince Andrew arrived on the island with a search and rescue helicopter. They were certainly making a big fuss over little old me.

Meanwhile, Case and Stormy were out before dawn on his sail-boat, as he was convinced that the cave would have an off-shore entrance. He was equally convinced that the entrance would be booby-trapped or guarded by underwater subversives with spear guns. The man obviously had an over-active imagination or watched too many movies.

Looking for Pest

In the end, they found me safe and sound. There was no nuclear device attached to the prison door and neither were there any subversives. The whole thing was a discount operation and the perpetrator and his cronies were all part of an amateur drama group called *The Friends of Oscar Wilde*. My confinement area was nothing but a disused munitions magazine and they hired the getaway car from Hertz. Some governments later repealed the discriminatory laws regarding gay marriage but that didn't help Justin and Jonathan, who were both sent down for twenty years for their part in the kidnapping. Mid-way through his term, Justin was transferred to a mental institution and Jonathan was released with time-off for good behavior. He ended up marrying one of the female prison guards and they lived happily ever after in Earl's Court.

We didn't have much time left for our holiday but managed to acquire a passable suntan before we returned to Oz. Some months later, we received the sad news that Chris Case had passed on. Stormy mentioned that he had often complained of feeling unwell but she thought that he was malingering in order to avoid his turn at scrubbing the deck. Surprisingly, the generous man left the vessel to Stormy in his will but the tax people moved in and confiscated it. Bloody bureaucracy!

You are probably wondering what we both are doing today and whether the relationship had legs. To tell you the truth, nothing has changed. Stormy is back where she belongs at Sam's Fly by Night Club and so am I, a lone figure at the bar. Why not drop by one evening and we could chew the fat and share a snack? They have some very nice red herrings on the bar menu.

THE MOUNTAINS OF MAYHEM

I was in a bit of a bind. My arms and legs were stretched beyond recommended tolerances and had been tied to four stakes that had been hammered into the sand. It was as hot as a chili sandwich, which was not surprising as the daylight temperature in the Gobi Desert can be uncomfortable. In the distance, I thought I heard the sound of a buzz saw. Could it be moving towards my favorite set of loins? Actually, I was delusional. It was just a family of flies heading in my direction.

Right here, right now, I should mention that Paddy Pest is an intrepid traveler and the stories that I tell you are harvested from all corners of the earth. People tell me that these tales are simply unbelievable and some of them even say this in a nice kind of way. I take any compliment that I can get. Now and then, I tend to stray from my central theme because sometimes I happen to stray from my original destination. Such a diversion was the reason that I ended up in such a sorry state in the Gobi Desert. Until then, I had never heard of Mönkhbat, the magnificent – Mongolia's answer to Donald Trump.

Mönkhbat was one of the tribal chiefs who held sway in this particular region. He was a giant of a man and his countenance was all the more distinctive because of a horrendous gash across his face. The legacy of a sword fight, the scar reached from under his eye and descended to an area below his lower lip. His supporters saw this disfigurement as a badge of courage.

His enemies saw him for what he was – a tyrant. Donald Trump used to fire people and so did Mönkhbat. He also burned their homes and barbecued their animals. He was so unpopular; it was surprising that he had six wives.

I was heading to India for the bi-annual conference of international secret agents and it was going to be as confusing as ever. Over three hundred John Smiths had signed on for the three day seminar. Bin Laden was going to give the key-note address on escape techniques but he bought the farm before he could escape. Such is life. Along the way, I thought I would look up my buddy Imran Khan, the cricketer turned politician. The travel people sent me to the birth place of Genghis Khan. I have really gone cold on these no-frills airlines.

I know that we all like to whine about airline travel but, really, these people have a lot of catching up to do. If they advertise air-conditioning, it means that there are no doors on the plane. Your seat companion is more than likely a duck or a goat. But what can you do? You are already in Business Class.

"Excuse me, Sir. Would you like a complimentary Yak's milk?"

My pal was in Mongolia, only last year, on bicycle would you believe? I can just picture him in the steppes of the high country with only his bike pump for company. In point of fact, he was there with a group and they all had back-up, including a Medevac team. I'm not like that. I'm a tough guy. Bring on snakes, spiders or rampaging elephants. I am good to go because I just love all that backs-to-the-wall kind of stuff.

However, when you are in an unfamiliar country with strange customs, you can often pull the wrong rein. In retrospect, I should never have gone all touchy-feely with the Mongol chieftain's wife. Because he had so many spouses, I didn't think that he would notice and she did have such a winning smile, a feat that is hard to achieve when you only have three teeth. Obviously, I had miscalculated the boundaries of Mongol hospitality and Mönkhbat had me on the sands of the Gobi as a reprisal – with no sunscreen. My dermatologist would have been livid. Had they never heard of Slip-Slop-Slap?

Those few hours that I spent pegged to the hot sand were the closest I have ever been to hell. The twine that bound my hands and feet felt like red hot rivets and my tongue was yearning for some neck oil (ice cold beer). One of the guards took time off from his sentry duty to tell me that there were red ants heading in my direction. What a nice guy!

Also heading in my direction was Ivana, the object of my affection and the fourth wife of the Mongol chief. I think that she must have had the whole harem in tow. They distracted the guard and freed me from bondage. Just in time! My deodorant was on its last legs.

The girls helped me with my escape route and there were many rivers to cross before I stumbled on a bus route that promised to take me to an airport and civilization as I knew it. Time was of the essence because, in my heart, I knew that the aggrieved husband would be seeking vengeance. After all, it had happened so many times before.

Once again, I was traveling on a wing and a prayer but I had shekels. Your money goes further if you are in an undeveloped country but sometimes the quality of service can be less than desirable. The Mongolian bus broke down five times during the journey and was finally towed into the terminus by an ox. As I alighted from the vehicle, the animal looked at me as if he was expecting a tip.

I have been described at various times by analytic people as being irreverent, irrational, irresponsible and alarmingly psychotic. I like to call on one of these descriptive characterizations when I am faced with a situation that has me distinctly off-side. I wondered if the tribal people of upper Mongolia were familiar with rude and ranting but evidently not. They thought that I wanted to buy something.

These kinds of places are a tough trek. Your patience will be tested and your dignity will be stripped bare, together with most of your spending money. You don't need to buy the trinkets that are on offer but, as you know, refusal often offends. In the situation that I was in, I figured that I needed as many friends as possible.

On the other hand, you should never over-extend your warmth and generosity to strangers, which often happens when you experiment with unknown alcoholic beverages. Like Paddy Pest, you may awake the morning-after in a fragile state of bewilderment.

I awoke to the most fearsome sight that I had ever seen – the grinning face of Mönkhbat, the magnificent. I was in a well furnished tent that obviously belonged to a buddy of his. It was also obvious that I was a prisoner. There were two guards on duty at the tent entrance. The alarm on my watch went off. My plane out of there would be departing in one hour but how would I get out of here? Paddy was in a pickle, once again.

Outside the tent, I heard a familiar grunting and shuffling noise. I have a friend who we call *The Ox* and he grunts just like that. He also does a very good Hunchback of Notre Dame impression but that's another story. I recognized this particular grunt. It was the ox that had towed us into town. It appears that he often performs this ritual and it is customary practice for the passengers to reward the animal with some vegetable matter on arrival. I was the only person on the bus to ignore him and I just knew that he could smell my fear through the thin canvas that separated us. He charged the tent.

What happened next was an exercise in futility. Oxen are not the smartest units on the planet and he got himself entangled in the canvas folds that fell down over my cowering self and also enveloped the two brutes on guard duty. I managed to slip away in the confusion that developed and headed for the airport and my original destination, where I was sure that cuckolded husbands were far more understanding.

It was all so different in Pakistan and India. I had accumulated all these friends who had been keeping my computer and utility services going for the past five years. Those individuals who work in call centers are just the nicest folks and I arrived with invitations for five weddings and a baptism in the River Ganges.

"We are thinking, Sahib, that we are calling our little fellow, Patrick. A small Mercedes would be an appropriate gift from the godfather."

Sadly, I couldn't make the baptism and Imran couldn't make our reunion, which was disappointing because he is a legend in his own lifetime. However, I did manage to take in the Khan Film Festival, which is a cavalcade of Bollywood movies. Not to be missed! The women in India and beyond are stunningly attractive. I didn't know how to keep track of all the beauties that I met so I took to dipping my finger in red ink and marking their foreheads. In that way, I knew that I had been there before Shane Warne.

Paddy Pest the traveler is a lot more relaxed than Paddy the detective. I am forever on my lunch break and rarely notice the dark people who lurk in the shadows. In case you think that this is a racist comment, I can assure you that my observation also applies to albinos, red-headed psychopaths and knife-throwing dwarfs. Nevertheless, there are other challenges that arise and one of these just happens to be related to lunch. I don't know what they put in the food in India but they just don't have enough toilets. You never know when nature will call.

I was learning the famed Indian Rope Trick and performing in front of dozens of spectators. I guess I was at least twenty feet up in the air with nothing holding up the rope. I then realized that nothing was also going to hold my Pork Vindaloo and spicy okra that I had recently consumed. Once again, Pest dissipates a crowd.

Although this episode was decidedly distasteful, it was nothing compared to my confrontation with the snake. Even though I sometimes make a show of bravado, I am really not that keen on reptiles and the invitation to go one-on-one with a cobra was terrifying. Only my pride prevented me from high-tailing it out of there.

Although my sponsor explained that snake charmers were a dying race, there is no fool like an old fool and I accepted the challenge. They gave me a basket and produced some kind of flute that was very similar to my friend's clarinet. Richard is a blow-hard of the finest pedigree. His efforts throughout the British Isles are legendary and I regarded it as an honor to receive tuition from him over a number of years. I was no expert but I could do a half-decent version of *Golden Wedding*. Unfortunately for the snake, this was all I could play.

The cobra is naturally a slow-moving serpent, although its initial strike reaction is fast and often fatal. Because traditional charm music is more Ravi Shankar than Woody Herman, the up-tempo jazz classic that I belted out really had him going double time. I don't think that anyone had ever seen a snake jump out of his basket before and the whole market area went ballistic. The amazing thing was that there were other snakes in other baskets and they popped out as well – all doing their own variations of Varsity Rag. I felt like the Pied Piper.

I am presently thinking that I will never be invited back to India again because I may well have upset the order of things. They don't like foreigners coming in and interfering with their traditions. Nevertheless, I have acquired a bit of a reputation around Sonagachi, the red-light district of Kolkata. They now call me Sugar Lips or Snake Eyes, depending on whether I am playing music or craps.

You may think that I had too much spare time on my hands and this may be true. The spy conference was a bit of a fizzer; especially when Bin Laden was replaced by David Copperfield. Most of the Americans went home after the first day. Nevertheless, it was a good time to catch up with an old adversary: Nadia Nikoff, the minx from Minsk.

"Hello darlink. Do you still 'ave that pop-gun in your pants?"

The agent provocateur was being provocative but it didn't bother me as I knew that she was keen on me. Let's face it. Who doesn't like Paddy Pest? I let her have my best wry grin and tried to be complimentary. "Nice to see you, again, Nadia. You appear to be ageing gracefully. Did you get that boob job done in New York?"

When you get two old foes together, the repartee never stops and so we made a night of it. The Bukhara restaurant is one of New Delhi's most famous and delights in serving its signature dish: Dal Makhani. The creamy butter gravy of black lentils and beans is full of ginger, garlic and other spices and, in this restaurant, the chefs simmer it for forty eight hours. Served with naan or chapati, they virtually have you eating out of their hand. If you wish to re-ignite an old flame, I always recommend an Indian restaurant.

Nadia was a bit nostalgic for the old days and so we toasted 'the cold war' with a plentiful supply of vodka. With each shot, the ardor in our respective breasts reached dangerous levels and I could foresee a situation where we would have to forgo dessert. And that Coconut Burfi looked sensational.

It never came to that. I had taken my eye off the ball and that can be fatal in my business.

The would-be assassin came at me with a flaming skewer of Chicken Tikki and if there hadn't been a crunchy pappadam on the floor, his attack would have been unannounced. We grappled in a fearsome display of male testosterone let loose. Tables and chairs were flying everywhere and the other diners were screaming in terror. Only Nadia retained her cool. She finished off the last of her vodka and then cracked her knuckles. Nothing or no-one was going to spoil her night out.

I was on the deck with my back on the floor. My assailant was on top of me and I could see the determination in those piggy eyes of his. His ugly face was contorted, distorted and yes, he snorted. Bugger me if he didn't look Mongolian.

That was about the end of it. Nadia stepped forward and let fly with a perfectly executed rabbit-chop. He rolled over and collapsed. She followed up with a kick into his wedding furniture and then effortlessly picked him up and threw him into the Tandoori oven. His screams frightened all the other diners and they fled the restaurant. Management was not pleased. The proprietor stepped forward and handed me a bill for the damage.

"Darlink! Are you all right?"

The tenderness of the KGB's most ruthless killer washed over me and almost diffused the ignominy that I felt about having been rescued by a woman, once again. I really must work on my martial-art skills. "Thanks, Nadia. I see that you haven't lost your touch."

"We need to get you into bed" she said with a wink.

As you know, a nod is as good as a wink to a blind man and I nodded enthusiastically. We retired to my hotel room and I am happy to say that Australia/Russia relations have never been better. As with these things, happiness is a fleeting moment and, the next morning, I awoke to a deserted bed and three empty vodka bottles. The bird had flown.

"Good morning, Sahib. My name is Vijay Pushkar. Can I drive you to the airport?"

My return journey home was going to be a direct flight, with a flight crew that I could trust – our local international carrier. My taxi trip to the airport was uneventful. Sure, Vijay tried to slash my throat with my credit card and a passing bus-driver hurled a flammable object into the cab but these are hurdles that Paddy Pest has to overcome on a daily basis. I settled comfortably into my business-class seat and surveyed the menu. I immediately felt uneasy. The main course was Mongolian Tandoori Hot Pot.

Did I mention that the steward was staring at me with his distinctive piggy eyes?

I was hoping to catch some well-earned shut-eye but there was no way that I was going to relax with a maniac on board. The steward also had a scar on his face, so he must have been a relative of Mönkhbat. The immigration policy of my country definitely has to be looked at.

A few hours into the flight, dinner had been served and there was no sign of the pig-eyed predator. He re-appeared when I went to the toilet. Can you imagine a more inappropriate place to have a dog-fight than in the confines of an airplane thunderbox? The thug must have been some kind of spider-man. He was somehow suspended from the ceiling when I closed the toilet door and dropped my pants. That's when he dropped on top of me.

Thank God for the security demands of the airline industry. They were now insisting on plastic cutlery and the Mongolian had a plastic knife in his mouth when he dropped. Nevertheless, he probably knew where to insert the blade for maximum effect. We slugged it out for a bit until an announcement came through the loud speaker. The aircraft was approaching severe air turbulence and there was only one seat-belt in the lavatory. It was already around me.

I don't know whether you have ever been through air turbulence while confined in a small space. You get bounced around quite a lot and the Mongol must have hit his head about a dozen times. He was just groggy enough to lose his equilibrium for a moment. In my business, a moment can be the difference between life and death.

I hadn't executed a spear tackle since the all-schools under-ten rugby final at Indooroopilly. I picked up the scar-faced monster and up-ended him into the toilet bowl. His cries of anguish were drowned by the sound of flushing water as he was sucked down through the outlet and into the atmosphere. As luck would have it, we were flying over the mountains of Mongolia at the time.

I hope he landed on Mönkhbat's house.

PEST AND THE PINNACLE OF POWER

It was always going to be difficult to rock up to the back door of the White House and ask to borrow half a cup of sugar. I was surprised that I got as far as I did. They spread-eagled me, patted me down and eventually asked the obvious question:

"What's with the empty cup?"

This question was directed at me as part of a routine fourteen hour interrogation that took place in a scream-proof room that was without windows or other creature comforts. Although there were only two interrogators, I had the feeling that there were about a dozen pairs of eyes analyzing every movement of my eyebrows.

The cup was being treated with kid gloves and had gone to forensics for evaluation. The report came back and indicated that it was a classic version of the Wedgewood Renaissance Gold range, valued at $48.50 and was probably stolen. There was no indication of any white powder residue, cyanide or Turkish coffee. They had to believe that I just wanted to borrow some sugar.

I was surprised that they didn't recognize me as this was my forty-seventh attempt to meet the President. Paddy Pest is not a man who gives up easily. The simple truth is that I was impressed with his idealistic rhetoric and just wanted to shake him by the hand. Is that too much to ask? In truth, I was probably profiled and when it was discovered that I was a foreigner, they probably didn't want to waste a handshake on somebody who couldn't vote.

It can be blustery in Washington and I had the distinct feeling that the winds of change were imminent. Contrary to my positive opinion of the Big Kahuna, dissatisfaction was in the air and I could tell from my run-in with the authorities that there were a lot of nervous people about. When they let me go, I decided to stay in town and do a bit of snooping. It is what I do best.

If you want to meet the President, there are a number of alternatives. To explore all possibilities, I believe that you can do no better than refer to the largest knowledge base in America: Hollywood. I vaguely remember seeing a movie where the bad lad (John Malkovich) was invited to a political fund-raiser on the back of a large donation that he had made to the President's re-election campaign. Of course, this low-life wanted to kill the President. I just wanted to shake hands with him.

What could be easier? Unfortunately, the fly in the ointment was the donation bit. Everybody knows that I am as tight as a fish's ass, so the prospect of them extracting any cash from me was bleak. I wondered if my charm would get me to first base. Thereafter, I would be able to ingratiate myself with the people that mattered.

Washington society demands that you be rich, famous, influential or full of bullshit. As I was ex-advertising, I had a degree in bullshit and was convinced that they would embrace whatever outrageous story I put forward in order to explain my fraudulent credentials. However, I was a pragmatist. One had to crawl a bit before you could even think of jumping into bed with an obscenely rich society spinster of questionable appearance. However, this was a party town and I wanted to be part of it.

"Excuse me, ladies. My name is Paddy Pest. Can you direct me to the nearest cuddle party, birthday bash or black-tie soirée. I'm in a celebration mood." They looked at me as if I were vermin and ran off. The word 'creep' filtered back through the humid atmosphere of a hot November night.

I didn't know much about my first invitation (which I had forged) but it was some charity organization that sends wetbacks back to their homeland. I wasn't familiar with these wetback people but I thought that it was sad that they were so far from home and away from their friends and family. I was later to learn that many of them already had their friends and relatives with them. The knees-up was some kind of beer and taco party and the host was a garrulous Texan senator. And you wouldn't believe it, he wore a sidearm. Many of you would know that I also carry a gun but I am very discreet about it. This joker was decked out like Wyatt Earp.

Needless to say, I didn't meet any obscenely rich spinsters at this function (other than the one that looked like Hoss Cartwright) and so I had to keep my powder dry. I was sure that an occasion would eventually present itself but I must say that I never expected more than I had bargained for. Enter the McDoodle twins.

Bonnie-Jo McDoodle and her sister Bonnie-Jean were twenty-five years of age and distantly related to a Scottish fast-food tycoon. The family was highly respected and seriously wealthy. This is probably one of the reasons that the girls were terribly spoiled and out of control. When I appeared on their radar, they must have been bored with the young studs that usually followed them around. Not that I would want to discount the fact that in my best duds with my stomach pulled in, I can look alarmingly attractive. I believe that they said it together.

"Yum!"

The McDoodle twins

It is always hard to separate twins and I didn't want to. The possibilities were mouth-watering. I introduced myself: Patrick Hamish Angus Alistair Pesticide – just call me Paddy.

"Hello Paddy," said Bonnie-Jo.

"We like you," said Bonnie-Jean and they both snuggled a little closer.

I have to say that my temperature started to rise, amongst other things. These were serious man-eaters and I was delighted to be on the menu.

It appears that the girls were indeed bored. We were at a gala ball to celebrate Gall-bladder Week and all the invitees were medical luminaries who had nothing better to talk about than their latest procedure. Daddy McDoodle was on the board of one of the hospitals and as Mrs McDoodle had run off with a corset salesman, the girls were needed to play hostess. Two for the price of one!

I am too refined to discuss my private peccadilloes but during my intimate sojourn with the girls, I asked them if they had ever been to the White House. They said no but they had been to a brown house on Embassy Row. I was getting closer but there was no hurry. The girls and I tripped around the party circuit for a number of weeks and they introduced me to a few movers and shakers. It was the kind of apprenticeship that one needed before entering the big stage, which I did on one fateful evening in November. It was a bitterly cold night but the lights were blazing in the mansion of John James Jitterbuck IV, the imperious newspaper magnate.

The private dinner party was supposedly for three hundred of his closest friends but, in reality, he didn't have any friends, so I scored an invite. My cover was that I was a famous Australian philanthropist who had just been awarded the Nobel Peace Prize for humanitarian works. I knew that the word *philanthropist* would arouse interest and my social availability was sure to reach the ears of those money-hungry leeches in the President's fund-raising unit. I could almost feel the carpet of the Oval Office under my feet. All I needed was approval from the Embassy staff.

"Mr Ambassador, I would like you to meet Patrick Pesticide from Australia. Paddy is here to further his relations with our Madam Secretary."

"Well, gee, Paddy! That's great. But don't forget to call on the Minister of Agriculture. You guys would have a lot to talk about."

What happened next was something that I am not proud of. I think that I may well have benefitted from some etiquette advice prior to my arrival but that's all very well after the fact, isn't it?

Fresh seafood had been flown in from Cape Cod and they had everything but cod. I was asked how the oysters compared with the Aussie version. Most people know that Sydney rock oysters are incomparable but

I didn't like to say that. I was half way through the digestive process and pondering the question when I had one of my now famous coughing fits. The oyster was immediately regurgitated and went sailing across the room and down the voluptuous décolleté of Mrs Jitterbuck's stunning cocktail dress. All conversation stopped immediately and the room remained embarrassingly silent. It then burst into uproar when I decided to try and recover the slippery morsel from the cavernous depths of you know where.

Mrs Jitterbuck's décolleté

As you might expect, this was a bit of a setback in my quest to find social acceptance in the nation's capital. The word got around that I was an uncouth individual and it is hard to shake these kinds of evaluations. I was removed from all Thanksgiving invite lists and even the McDoodle twins started avoiding me. My holiday dinner at the Ankara All-Nite Café was a lonely affair although the staff did their best to cheer me up. Bibi, the belly dancer was an up-front kind of chick but I have to tell you; it looked like Paddy Pest was the one who had laid an egg.

I haven't mentioned it before but there was a fall-back position if the philanthropist gig didn't eventuate. It would be one of the biggest challenges of my life – to become a national hero in two weeks. I had put the pressure on myself because I wanted to be back in Oz for an important horse race and the Prez was booked out on a goodwill tour a few days before that. However, he couldn't leave the country without shaking hands with the man who saved the nation from shame and ridicule or perhaps single-handedly thwarted another Al Qaeda terror plot. Since Bin Laden's death, revenge was in the air.

There have been a number of sightings of Osama in America, since his apparent demise and I wondered if he had a twin brother. One such informant saw him getting on a bus with Elvis only last year but the idiot couldn't remember which route it was. I don't know many Muslim folks apart from Bin Ali, who has also bin Cassius Clay but we don't talk much these days. In fact, he may well have passed on for all I know. Still, there's no point in calling yourself a detective if you don't detect. I therefore chose to sniff around a few mosques and kebab joints.

The smell was distinctly revolutionary at the first mosque that I attended. The music was quite mesmerizing and I wondered if there were any subliminal messages being transmitted other than the *Eat at Akmar's* jingle that seemed to reach out to many of the ghetto residents. Akmar's was a popular eating place because the owner liked jazz but the food was terrible and the hygiene was questionable. You went there if you wanted Salmon Ella Fitzgerald.

You also went there if you wanted information, disinformation or unsubstantiated rumor. Could I slip into the place without looking like an infidel in a three-piece suit? No, I couldn't, so I pretended to be a jazz connoisseur who had just discovered Preservation Hall. I ordered a small glass of Arak and settled down to enjoy the music. This masquerade worked a treat until I took my first sip of the strong liquor. Whatever they gave me, it made me dizzy. I woke up in a garbage skip, not far from the café. I could still hear the muted sound of Mr Gillespie and his trumpet in the distance. So much for that plan.

"Come on Paddy. Use your brain. There's got to be a solution somewhere."

I often talk to myself. It gives me the motivation to keep going but

I have to say that this project was proving a little difficult. I wondered if Dabs Berkenschmidt could help.

Dabs had come to MGM with some of the European New Wave creative people and had won a Golden Eyebrow Pencil as a make-up artist. Eventually, his garlic breath became a bit of a problem and his popularity began to wane. Rather than pension him off, the studio let him finish his days in the wardrobe and props division. Being an old soldier, he had already met the big man at a veteran's parade. Of course, he didn't tell him that he had been fighting for Hitler.

"Dabs! What can you do to help me get close to the President? I know that you have the power. Think movies and you're sure to come up with something."

Dabs had an encyclopedic mind as far as the cinema was concerned and he soon honed-in on the Frederick Forsyth nail-biter, *The Day of the Jackal*. He would just upgrade the conflict circumstance.

"Vell, Paddy, ve can paint some gray to the 'air, add a mustache, chop off an arm or a leg and put some medals to the chest. There you 'ave it: a Vietnam veteran."

I wasn't so keen on the amputee angle but otherwise agreed on the idea. When Veterans Day arrived, I could see merit in the Berkenschmidt thought process. All the disabled people had front row seats. I would have to attract the President's attention from three rows back. Should I scream out "Rape" or "Bomb" or just announce that I was his love child?

In the end, I didn't have to do any of that. I just broke wind and the assembly scattered in seconds. I was left standing man to man with the power prince of the greatest nation in the world. Once the offending air-space between us was diffused, he boldly strode over to where I was standing. There was so much that I wanted to say but my mouth wasn't working. He calmly produced a packet of peppermints and handed me one. I think that our hands touched so I definitely consider that a handshake.

He just said "keep yourself nice" and walked off.

PEST LOSES HIS MARBLES

There didn't seem to be much confusion about the seating arrangements. Her Majesty was in her usual spot at the head of the table and her consort was opposite. The kids and their respective wives shuffled along to their designated positions, sat down and tucked in. The last remaining place was for me, Paddy Pest.

It wasn't a very popular win when I ran off with the *Better Homes and Gardens* lottery, the first prize being an invitation to share Hogmanay with the Royal Family. You know, with me being an Aussie interloper and all that. Needless to say, I do take umbrage with this desultory rejection of my patriality. Being a long-standing member of the Commonwealth, Australians retain a strong affinity with the Crown and her subjects. I wasn't backward in telling Her Madge all of that, so we got on like a house on fire. We touched on the subjects of sun, surf, white beaches, fresh seafood and cricket. Unfortunately, there was an ugly silence when she advised me that they would not be serving any prawns, this year.

I have never quite taken to the taste of Haggis. It's not that I don't like eating intestines. I think that the fact that it is cooked in a sheep's stomach is mildly off-putting. Having said all that, I can now tell you that the Royals woofed it down like there was no tomorrow. We had afters in the drawing room and I was able to reconnect with our noble ruler, all the more noble because she was a horse-racing fanatic, just like me. The fact that Paddy Pest shared ownership in a horse called Distant Ruler tickled her fancy. I promised to tip her into it, next time he ran.

The day ended with kisses and fond farewells and everybody promised to write, although I would not be holding my breath. One set of guards marched me to another set of guards and before I knew it, I was back on the streets. I immediately regurgitated the Haggis and headed for a nearby fast-food outlet that declared itself *The Codfather*. Wasn't it fish and chips that made Britain great?

It turns out that I was being followed. Somebody had put a tail on me. When you have as much experience as I have, you can always flush out a rank amateur. The incompetent stalker was leaning on a lamp-post, reading a newspaper that was upside-down. He was probably with the CIA or Scotland Yard. I am not a bad person although I sometimes do bad things. That is why the spooks always like to know where I am and what I am doing.

"If that Australian idiot is loose in this country, I want to know about. Is that clear?"

"Yes, Sir," said the MI5 lackey, who was used to his boss's perpetual rants. The covert undercover team was always delighted with these kinds of jobs. The places where Paddy Pest frequents were never far from a pub or a house of ill-repute.

Paddy Pest is also often involved with foreign bodies and, in this instance, I had a brief from somebody else's king and country. My mission, should I accept it, was to recover the Parthenon Marbles from the British Museum and return them to their rightful owners, the Greek Government. The fish and chip shop was a safe house where I could receive my instructions and the Greeks had been cunning and clever. They had put in an Indian family to manage the Hake and Halibut.

Evidently, Lord Elgin, who was some kind of English git, purloined the artifacts from their home at the Acropolis in the early nineteenth century. Continuous political representation has done little to mend the acrimony between the two governments and the obvious solution was to bring in Paddy Pest. Of course, I had no idea that the bloody things were so large and would have reneged on the deal if I had not lost my cash advance on the three-thirty at Kempton Park. Why do I continue to support slow horses?

Normally, I work alone but, given the magnitude of the task and the fact that the marble was stuck to the wall, I had to get some help. There was only one thing to do: become a Mason.

This is not as simple as it sounds. I went all over London with this funny handshake and people thought that I was bonkers. Eventually, I met a chap who took me to his Lodge for the initiation ceremony. They blindfolded me, stripped me bare and shoved a feather up my ass. It was so degrading. After a bit more mumbo jumbo, I became a member of the brethren.

If you are a Freemason, other Masons will do anything for you so it wasn't long before I had assembled a gang for the big heist. On paper, the plan looked good. We would sneak into the museum after closing, strip down the marble and assemble it in overnight suitcases. Multiple taxi cabs would ferry the luggage over to Victoria Station in time to catch the last train to Brighton. Waiting for us would be a small fishing boat that would then return the prize back to Athens. The vessel would be manned by Cypriot sailors and be flying a flag of convenience.

"Hey bro, what's that flag with a picture of a toilet on it?"

"That's a flag of convenience. Don't you know anything?"

It all seemed so easy but I am a perfectionist and I decided on a dry run. I substituted some cement slabs that I had found in the basement area of the B&B where I was staying. Everything was fine until they loaded the concrete onto the boat, which immediately sank. Most inconvenient! We had to lay low for a while so I decided to move camp, which was most fortuitous. Somebody had messed with the building's foundations and the B&B completely fell down the day after I left.

As everybody knows, the star of Mykonos is a great footballer but he is also a valuable reservist with the Greek army: their go-to man whenever trouble presents itself. I didn't ask for any help but they figured that I might need it. He would be able to tell the difference between the Elgin Marbles and the Moaning Lisa. The museum was doing a short season of French pornography.

I don't think that Milos had ever met any Masons before but he immediately made them feel at ease with his gregarious manner and generous sense of humor. I sent him off on a few reconnaissance missions but he always ended up at a pub near Stamford Bridge or White Hart Lane. Although he was lazy, he did have influence and a large navy frigate arrived in Brighton Harbor to replace the fishing vessel. It was disguised as a cruise ship.

Eventually, the enthusiastic crew of Masons hit the British Museum on a cold night in January. The security staff was watching *Britain's Got Talent* and Susan Boyle was drowning out the sound of the jackhammers.

The marble had been detached from the walls and this is where I took my eye off the ball and made a vital mistake. The taxis had all arrived and I delegated the loading responsibility to a chap called Michael Mary Martin Murphy, aka Mad Mick. Milos and I retired to a nearby ice-cream shop to share a Banana Mouskouri.

"Well, Milos, how have you enjoyed your stay in London?" It was a rhetorical question that was no more than a silence buster but he responded vigorously.

"Very much, Paddy! The girls are all very friendly and the football is wonderful. One day, I hope to return to play for Chelsea or Fulham." I couldn't help but feel that if we stuffed up this job he would be playing for Wormwood Scrubs.

On completion of the taste treat, we caught a taxi to Victoria Station to once again take charge of the consignment. When nothing or no-one was sighted after thirty minutes, we blamed the traffic. After one hour, we blamed Mick Murphy. Unbeknown to us, the cabs had been diverted to King's Cross Station and the priceless artifacts were en route to Liverpool. They would soon be half way across the Irish Sea. The bloody IRA!

I expect that before the alarm bells stopped ringing at the British Museum, MI5 and the Coast Guard would be all over the country, searching for the stolen treasure. They would not bring in any outside agencies because the loss of the Elgin Marbles would be a great embarrassment. The museum closed this section of the building, citing refurbishment. Obviously, this was not good for business but, fortunately, traffic picked up at the French pornographic exhibition.

I had covered my tracks and was confident that the Brits would not rumble me. However, things would not be so rosy back in Athens and I feared for my safety. I slipped away into the countryside with the Greeks right behind me. This was pretty scary stuff. No-one wants the Greeks up their ass.

"We are looking for a man with a guilty look on his face. If you assist us with our enquiries, we will reward you with tickets to a forthcoming Demis Roussos concert."

They received absolutely no help, whatsoever and I disappeared into the foggy dew of the North Country. Then something strange happened.

A week after the robbery, MI5 were on the phone, asking if I would participate in the effort to recover the stolen masonry. What could I say? I had my suspicions and I advised them that the instigator of this abominable action was extremely clever, highly intelligent and very cunning. Perhaps it wasn't the IRA, after all. Nevertheless, I made the crossing to Ireland, disguised as a tourist. I kissed the Blarney Stone, chased leprechauns with the Americans and consumed vast quantities of Guinness. Sometimes my workplace isn't too bad.

There was no electronic chatter to speak of but I was hearing plenty of gossip in the south of the country. Evidently a lot of the tourist attractions were decaying due to the limited lifespan of their basic material. Most of them were made of cork in Cork but this material was now on the nose. Even the wine companies were using screw-tops and the traders were hurting. The council came to an arrangement with a local lad to build some historic marble monuments. This is when things started to smell a bit.

Everything pointed to a chap called Frank the Wog. Two hundred years earlier, his great grandfather, Francesco, came to this country. He was an Italian stonemason and after a short courtship, married Veronica the Virgin. The Irish have a habit of maintaining these sobriquets for a little longer than they should. Every first born son was called Frank the Wog.

I didn't have to do much. I fingered Frank to the Guardia and they pounced at dawn, which is what they do. The Elgin Marbles were found in his vegetable patch amongst his impressive collection of garden gnomes. Evidently, his usual marble supplier had come up short and Frank's contract with the Cork Council looked shaky. It was a bold plan and I would have liked to punish Mad Mick for his part in it but I had to protect my own interests.

In the end, the Marbles were returned to the British Museum and no one was the wiser. For my part, there was talk of a knighthood but I am still waiting. A shame, really! It would have been nice to catch up with Queenie again.

MURDER AT THE BLUE CRAB CAFE

It was my first rocket launch at Cape Canaveral and I was honored. They don't usually like outsiders around when they are pushing all their little buttons, so this was a tribute to my standing within the community. You know how it is. They get all these dumb questions that detract from the job at hand. So, I decided to circumvent the PR person and try and find the loo on my own. I turned left instead of right but, nevertheless, there it was: the traditional symbol for the water closet. I must say that I didn't take much notice of the addendum that indicated that this facility was for crew only.

The crew must have been made up of very small people because this privy was extremely compact. All the same, I unhitched my strides and went to work. I don't know how long I was there but all of a sudden I heard and felt a mechanical noise and the whole room started to move.

"Hey guys, wait a minute. I haven't finished, yet."

I reckon we must have gone at least half a mile when the room stopped sliding sideways and started elevating. There were no windows but we seemed to be pretty high. A few more clinks and clunks and it seemed that I had been deposited somewhere. I was reading a very illuminating article on artificial insemination, so I decided to finish it before pulling on my pants, checking my tie and walking out into a cylindrical hallway. It was then that I heard the countdown.

I don't know how many of you have been in a spacecraft in the final throes of countdown but the overriding emotion is stark terror. I think that it was the boss astronaut who turned around to see who was screaming and aborted the take-off with two seconds to spare.

"Holy Moses, Ralph! We've got a stowaway."

Paddy Pest was not a popular chappy. You just can't stop these procedures and immediately start again. We were all driven back to the scramble room. Then they discovered that the toilet was blocked and the weather rolled in, didn't it?

In all, the launch was delayed ten days and the extra cost was approximately twenty-seven million dollars. When I asked them if they would take a check, they didn't think it was funny. I was escorted from the grounds and, yes, my invitation for egg-nog with the base commander was rescinded.

You may wonder what I was doing on the space coast. I was there because it was near Melbourne, which is where I live, except that I live in Melbourne, Australia. The stupid travel agent had sent me to Melbourne, Florida.

Please let me vent my feigned displeasure. I was actually delighted to be in Florida and immediately headed down to Miami and South Beach, where their art-deco buildings are without comparison. At night, the place lights up and the al fresco diners share the footpath with hot babes, cool dudes and freaks of all description.

"I think that you will enjoy our outdoor setting, Sir. Our patrons like to commune with the street traffic. You never know who you might see."

I was about to plunge into my first course, which looked most appetizing, when two pavement artists camped next door to my table. Each produced a gigantic python, which slithered around their bodies and tried to engage with the passing parade. Well, one did, anyway. The other one hit my entrée like a whip crack at a country rodeo. Oh, how I wished that I still had that Cape Canaveral toilet with me because my crap went everywhere. The medical people found me in the gutter in a complete state of shock. They eventually dusted me off and I recovered my seat. The snake charmers were moved on but not before the waiter had placed a small notice on my table that read: *Please don't feed the animals.*

It takes a lot to terrify Paddy Pest and, here, in the space of a few days, I had been completely rattled, twice. Thank God it wasn't a rattlesnake. Bourbon is always a good relaxant in situations like this, so I picked up a quart on the way back to my motel. It was the only thing to do.

My down-market sleeping quarters were a haven for the kind of bimbos that give bimbos a bad name. They were congregating near the driveway entrance and I knew that it would be a tortuous path to my room.

"Hi there, handsome. Would you like to party with little 'ole Cindy Lou?"

In point of fact, Cindy Lou was actually Conchita Consuelo Gonzales, an undercover cop with Miami Vice. Everybody knew that but me. Whenever there was a bust, she was always on the front page of the newspapers with the notation 'Conchita Gonzales, undercover policewoman.' I don't know why she bothered decking herself out as a hooker although I must say that she scrubbed up pretty well. She had come-hither eyes, voluptuous lips and a very nice ass. No wonder I never made it to my room. Have I mentioned that she could also drink?

Before the negotiation was over, the bourbon was gone and we found ourselves at *The Petrified Pelican,* a night club of some notoriety in downtown Miami. I liked broads that could hold up their end and I knew that she liked me. She liked me even better when she discovered a bunch of C notes in my wallet. I could tell that the gal was suspicious because if you've got that kind of money, you don't stay at the kind of fleapit where I was holed up. What she didn't know is that's why I've got that kind of money.

I suppose that I could have been Mafia. Even a Cuban revolutionary, at a pinch! I told her that I knew people in high places but she was having none of that. I also told her that she had a nice ass and that was enough provocation to buy another ten dollar bottle of champagne for eighty big ones. We were both bubbling over with goodwill. Things became a little fuzzy after that. If we had sex, it was forgettable because I couldn't remember a thing. I awoke with a hangover, stretched across my coin-in-the-slot vibrating bed. My wallet was intact and my clothes were not in disarray. All power to the Miami police!

If you come to Florida, you just have to go to the track. Their signature racecourse, Gulfstream Park, was closed, so I sobered up and headed for Calder Park. There are always ten winners somewhere on any given day and my wallet was still full of C notes.

The racetrack is a haven for people of low moral fiber and there were degenerates everywhere. Manny the Dip, Nice Albert, Slops Malone, Marvin Morganstein and Christina with Balls were all there. I was particularly impressed with Christina. She was about sixteen stone, wore loose fitting clothes and her communication skills, although offensive, were brutally flamboyant.

"G'day asshole," she intoned. So Australian, I thought.

It was hard to leave Christina with Balls. She had given me a tip which won by seven lengths. The jockeys of the three fancied runners all fell off. This kind of information is priceless.

"This one is for you, Paddy. The nag hasn't won in thirty-five starts. It is badly weighted and the pundits don't give it a chance." She was right. This is exactly the type of animal that usually gets me in. This time, we struck the mother lode. I wondered what Christina might want in return. I shuddered at the thought.

I suspect that some of you may be a little bored with my mundane travels through Florida. Wherever Paddy Pest goes, there is usually mystery, excitement and a whole lot of action. You have to remember that I am on holidays and the fact is that Florida is God's waiting room for countless gamblers, gangsters and other elderly brethren. Their action days are over although the crime statistics still boast over five hundred murders every year. Of course, I had to stumble in on one of them.

"Paddy, why don't you take some extra time-out and see our West Coast? It is quite lovely at this time of year. There is a terrific boat festival at Naples and the golf courses are first class."

"Thanks, Conchita. That sounds good. You're not trying to get rid of me, are you?"

The direct route to the West Coast, the road known as Alligator Alley, is a hundred-mile trip through the Everglades. It is as straight as an arrow and the comfort stops are minimal. The alternative scenic route is called the Tamiami Trail and takes you past the very disturbing Skunk Ape Research Headquarters. I preferred to pull into a charming mirage called Joanie's Blue Crab Café at Ochopee. It is just down the road from the smallest post office in America.

The place wasn't unlike Alice's Restaurant. You can get anything you want at Joanie's. The lady herself is a gregarious person and her patter is only restricted by a lack of customers. When she said that they had an outdoor area, I took advantage of a break in conversation, grabbed an ice-cold Corona and headed for the grassy area that sloped down to the swamp. There didn't appear to be any alligators around, although I did hear some rippling in the reeds.

You wouldn't believe what happened next. I found a lady's gold Rolex watch.

On closer examination, I discovered that it was still wrapped around the lady's wrist. Her forearm had been severed just below the elbow near the funny bone. I'll bet she didn't think that it was so funny. I decided not to make a fuss and slipped the watch into my pocket and returned inside. Joanie had my Gator Burger on the griddle and those onion rings smelled like heaven for breakfast. You just can't beat fried onions in the morning.

"Tell me, Joanie. Can you remember who might have been outback in the last few days?"

She bunched up her pert little nose and tried to think. It looked painful.

"I don't know, Hon. It's been raining a lot, this week and most of my customers like to keep dry. Although, there were those two heavy dudes from the city! They had a loud dame with them. She was a very colorful dresser."

No, she couldn't recall whether the girl came back inside with them or not. Why wouldn't she? The description of the two stand-over men was vague but one of them had to be Nice Albert, one of the degenerates that I met at the track. She had no trouble describing the lass. For some reason, a woman can describe another woman and her clothes and accessories right down to her toe-nail polish. In my mind, there was no doubt about it. Nice Albert and his sidekick had thrown Lady Gaga to the alligators.

The pond behind the Blue Crab Café

Conchita Gonzales had been good to me so I decided to throw the lady a bone. Within an hour, the detective and a forensics team arrived by helicopter. They scoured the swamp for evidence but only came up with some very colorful clothing. The lady's dress was neither appropriate for the climate nor bite-proof.

Surprisingly, the Miami-Dade Police Department was not that keen to pursue this case with much enthusiasm. There was only one eighteen-year-old tea lady in their building who was a Gaga fan. Often, in situations like this, they try and handball the job to an incompetent who is not likely to get a result. In fact, that's how I scored the consultancy job.

I trolled the cheap motels around the start of U.S. highway eighty-four and even followed a lead to Key Largo but there was nothing there except the ghosts of Bogie and Bacall. In the end, the victim wasn't Lady Gaga at all but Nice Albert's third wife, Daisy, who was a colorful character in her own right. The mobster was looking good for his wife's murder and if you needed a precedent, I will tell you that neither of his previous spouses is alive today.

Nice Albert is a bit of a misnomer. He really isn't a very nice person.

In his youth, he had cut up rough around the Chicago underworld with his switchblade knife. Then there were those years in Sing Sing, the jail for show business people. Johnny Cash went to prison. Merle Haggard, Gary Glitter and Leonard Cohen all spent time in striped pajamas and Albert knew them all. Nevertheless, he couldn't abide anyone who would sing to the cops. Was that Daisy's sin?

"You're a rat-fink, Albert Benevolenti. I've given you the best years of my life and you treat me like a two-bit hooker." Evidently, Daisy could dish it out and sometimes she took no prisoners. "I've a good mind to let the boys at Miami-Dade know exactly what you've been up to. Just see if I don't."

When details of Albert's latest dastardly deed were described in the dailies, the general public was outraged. Daisy was a popular member of *The Risqué Rockettes*, a high-kicking dance troupe that was well known around the night spots of Miami. The gal had also been a half-decent sports star in Colorado, when she first met Nice Albert. I believe that she played ice hockey with Martina Navratilova for the Aspen Mother Puckers.

I think that it was Edison who said that genius is 1% inspiration and 99% perspiration. It is the same with police work and the culmination of this case was very much down to perspiration. The temperature had climbed to over one hundred degrees when the air-conditioning in the interrogation room went down. We had to open the windows.

By the way, did I tell you that Daisy owned a parrot? His name was Clive and he was a very cheeky parrot. The bird was very loyal and only left her side for food and more food. It goes without saying that he would hit the road if there was an issue of self-preservation. Such an issue arose when Nice Albert and his sidekick threw Daisy to the alligators. Clive freaked out and flew off.

In the interrogation room, we were having a hard time pinning the crime on the smug, arrogant repeat offender who was sitting in front of us, grinning. Angel, his sidekick, had proved to be an unreliable witness. Suddenly, we discovered that there had been another observer of the crime, who presented himself with a swish and a squawk. The recorder kept running.

I couldn't believe it when Clive the parrot flew in through the open window and settled on my shoulder. My cheeky assistant claimed that all I needed was an eye-patch to look like a fearsome Long John Silver. Anyway, Daisy's feathered friend didn't let up. He glared at Nice Albert and continually squealed:

"You did it. You did it. Clive wants a cracker. You did it."

It was just what we needed. Gonzales recorded the bird's statement and I gave him a cracker. We read Albert his rights. He immediately broke down and confessed which was just as well. When we replayed the eye-witness account, we couldn't understand a word that the macaw said.

As a thank you for my efforts, Conchita invited me and the parrot out to dinner and you wouldn't believe it, we were given that same table next to the pythons. This time, the hungry snake didn't bother with the entrée – he went straight for the bird. Clive disappeared into the bowels of the slimy creature. Enough was enough. Gonzales flashed her badge and called in Animal Rescue. The reptile was escorted off the premises and, in the absence of the third party, Conchita and I decided to miss dessert and make it an early night – at her place.

As we passed the snake charmer, I slipped him my last C note.

Thank God that parrot is gone.

PRIDE – A SMALL COUNTRY IN AMERICA

Some of my relatives were thespians in the early days of Hollywood and gained some notoriety by being continually plagued by bad reviews for overacting. Many of my current friends have been similarly embarrassed but they wouldn't want to live anywhere else. I try and visit them whenever I am on the West Coast.

"Well, blow me down if it isn't Mr Pest. Welcome back to LA, Sir. Would you like your usual room with the vibrating bed? By the way! How is your back pain, these days?"

Pest usually comes to Los Angeles at the behest of one of the security organizations. Because they are continually ravaged by internal politics, the powers that be often like to bring in external consultants and I am very cheap.

"Let's get that Pest guy over here. He knows where all the bodies are buried and doesn't charge overtime. Just make sure that you lock up your daughters."

I was at a party for shirt-lifters in Santa Monica and, I have to say, Monica would have been aghast if she had known of the shenanigans that went on in her saintly patch. This soiree wasn't totally offensive but they were snorting cocaine and performing lewd acts. Don't even ask me about the malicious gossip and character assassinations. What is it about insecure people that they have to mouth-off about their friends the way they do? I only joined in to be sociable.

I had passed myself off as a journalist for a gay celebrity magazine and my date for the night was Elton John. We arrived in a super-charged pumpkin and had completely blown them away. After all, it was Halloween and with Elton you can't do things by halves.

Snatch McArdle had survived five box-office bonanzas in a row and there were teenage girls all around the world who hyper-ventilated every time he opened his mouth. They were not aware that he played for the other side and no-one was about to tell them. Certainly, not me!

The fact that Snatch fancied me was probably down to my grooming consultant, who had tutored me in the art of exfoliation and my skin was crying out for peer approval. The young man approached me with a plate of rude food, which were the only vittles on offer. I felt distinctly uneasy. If Elton saw how he was fawning over me, I would not be catching the Pumpkin Express home that evening. To tell you the truth, the shindig was rather tedious and I was hanging out for a cold beer and a 'burger, served with loving care by a valued representative of the Hooters restaurant franchise. There was never going to be any clandestine plot hatched within these walls so I hit the road.

How wrong can you be?

The first inkling that anything was amiss was when the city of Chula Vista blew up. Chula Vista is half way between San Diego and the Mexican border. The sad thing was that nobody noticed for three days. I expect that the extremists targeted the seventh largest city in Southern California because of its rating by *Forbes Magazine* as one of the ten most boring places in America. This was just a dry run. They were proving what could be done without upsetting anyone. Their demands would surely follow.

When the police in downtown San Diego finally heard about the catastrophe, it took them no time at all to cover the seven miles to what was left of Chula Vista. The whole place was a crime scene and they were all over it. I hooked up with one of their youngest and brightest, Lupita Gonzales. I asked her if she had a sister in uniform in Miami.

"I have seven sisters, Mr Pest but none of them live in Florida."

I liked this gal. She had a measure of respect for her elders but as we were going to be working together, I didn't want any of that formal crap. "Hey, kid. Just call me Paddy."

Sifting through the wreckage was time-consuming but the bomb squad had managed to isolate three possible locations as ground zero. On investigation, it was discovered that all three sites were on short rental to the Boom Boom Corporation, a shady, off-shore organization that was heavily into manufacturing. Although there were a number of shelf companies listed under their corporate umbrella, there were others that were extremely active. What would you say if I told you that their top-of-the-line products were Fag Cigarettes, Chocolate Queens and Gaytime Ice-cream? It wasn't long before I found a listing for one of their smaller operations. Their advertising slogan said it all: *Rude Food for You, Dude?*

I couldn't believe my eyes. The address of the CEO was in Santa Monica, California – an address I knew very well. With Gonzales and most of the LAPD in tow, I descended on the seaside bungalow with great enthusiasm. Paddy Pest was about to make a name for himself. Unfortunately, we missed the bad guy by thirty minutes and I was hauled over the coals for allowing Lupita to divert me to a bra sale, en route to the confrontation. To be fair, some of the girls in the SWAT team encouraged her and also took time off.

I have never been a fan of board games but I knew that we were back to square one. Then again, perhaps not! We had narrowed the list of possible perpetrators to four per cent of the population. I have a friend in advertising that refuses to ignore demographics and it seemed that the destruction of Chula Vista was a gay retaliation for something or other. I know that they don't like boring but surely it had to be more than that?

In the meantime, the President was updated and Gonzales and I were flown up to the White House for a personal briefing. The great man and I had met before for a short time but I don't think that he would have remembered. Lupita instantly hit it off with the First Lady, especially when she told her all about the bra sale. I also had some time with the Joint Chiefs of Staff but they were not so friendly.

"Who is this guy and what kind of accent is that?"

Their immediate reaction was to bomb one of the Mardi Gras marches but I felt that this was severe, as most gays were patriots. Plan B had more going for it but there seemed no justification to bomb Alaska, although it might warm up the place a bit. I assured them that the investigation was in good hands and they should take a step backwards and breathe deeply. It was good to get out of there.

"Tell me, Paddy. Who do you think these people are? Are they a serious threat to our way of life?"

"I don't know Mr President but they sure as hell don't like boring. If I was you, I would hold off on any speechmaking for the time being."

The tyrants were certainly not boring and they brought their fight close to home when they finally unveiled their demands in a most unusual manner. I don't know what the early morning commuters must have thought when they arrived at the National Mall to discover that a huge condom was completely covering the Washington Monument.

"Holy guacamole, Virginia. Is that what I think it is?"

"It certainly is, Dick. I wonder if it's a promotion for safe sex."

Safe sex, indeed! It wasn't even safe to climb up that damn obelisk to retrieve the slippery sheath and you all know which bunny drew the short straw for that little task. At least, I was the first to be able to read their demands, which were inscribed on the side of the condom.

They called themselves the Grand Alliance of Young Sophisticates and they were pissed-off. Yes, the gay revolution had finally arrived. There was nothing for it but to arrange a think tank in the Oval Office. The Joint Chiefs were there as was a select Senate committee and Joel Silvertail, the First Lady's hair stylist. We might need an opinion from the other side.

Their demands were quite simple. They wanted their own country and they wanted it on American soil. They already had San Francisco. These were greedy people.

The Minister for the Interior suggested that we give them the bone yard in the Mojave Desert. The bone yard was a gigantic scrapheap of decaying airplanes that was already a blot on the landscape and new owners could only improve it. I liked his thinking but someone had to explain to him that all gays aren't flight attendants. Someone suggested Paris, Texas. It certainly sounded sophisticated.

Although he was barely speaking to me after I had departed the Santa Monica party, I gave Elton a call and asked if he knew anything about this. He hedged a bit but finally confessed that he had first option on building an entertainment complex, to be called *The Liberace*.

All this may sound ridiculous but in truth, it had already happened before. In Western Australia, a disgruntled ratepayer rebranded himself as Prince Leonard of Hutt River Province. On behalf of himself and his eighteen thousand acre property, he seceded from the Commonwealth. In 1976, the post office refused to handle mail addressed to Hutt River and the tax department was also on his hammer. Prince Leonard declared war on

Australia but decided to cease hostilities a few days later. Both government departments relented and Hutt River is now a Commonwealth tax-free zone. He issued his own stamps and coins and built up an incredible supporter base. There are now some thirty permanent residents of Hutt River and up to eighteen thousand overseas citizens. The official languages of the principality are English, French and Esperanto.

Having said all this, I might mention that those in the Oval Office had completely failed to acknowledge the elephant in the room. They seemed oblivious to the fact that the plotters had nuclear capability. They had already sequentially listed their targets and there were few surprises: New York, Boston, Chicago and Toledo, Texas. The bomb maker had been involved in a road rage incident in Toledo and had been the subject of some politically incorrect abuse. Tough titty, Toledo!

We had a new team member. Ms Bernardo was a savvy profiler, who had come on board because of her experience with gang related violence. Maria was quite a beauty and hailed from the west side of New York City. Lupita had decided that she wanted to return to San Diego (it was sale time) and so I joined forces with Maria and we went to the Big Apple.

Lupita goes shopping.

This was a crucial appointment as the lady was a New Yorker and knew that all the locals were very sensitive concerning air-borne attacks. However, she was adamant that we had time on our side and was confident that there would be no action until the Broadway revival of La Cage Aux Folles was over. The strategy would be to keep bums on seats and extend the season, if need be.

Homeland Security had put us up at a very nice hotel but, immediately, I noticed that something was wrong – there were no valets. Most of the waiters were missing and there was no prissy desk clerk to receive us. The gays were all leaving town.

I found a booking for Mr and Mrs Smith and proceeded to process our own registration. I even managed an upgrade to the Honeymoon Suite. Surprisingly, Maria did not object. The hotel was quite full and I suspected that few people were aware of their forthcoming annihilation. I wondered if I had time for a haircut.

When the re-groomed Paddy Pest arrived back in our room, it was evident that the profiler was on top of things. I like an assertive woman. Her white board was overflowing with photos, calculations, formulas and cross-references. You have to cover a lot of parameters when you profile someone and this job was as difficult as any that I have seen. Nevertheless, she had come up with an astounding conclusion regarding the Grand Alliance of Young Sophisticates – they all liked show tunes.

This revelation hit me like a ton of bricks and, contrary to her first analysis, I knew that we had little time to spare. We had two options:

a) Immediately rush over to 42nd Street and apprehend these monsters or

b) Take a short nap and then head over to Broadway. It had been a long day.

I don't intend to go into details regarding the short nap but we both arrived at the entertainment precinct fresh and eager. But was it too late? The lights of the theater district had been dimmed and we were rocked out of our socks when we saw the billboard outside the Longacre Theater: *La Cage Aux Folles – production suspended until further notice.*

My eagle eye picked up on a speck of a light that seemed to be coming from the bowels of the building. We un-holstered our weapons and entered through the stage door. The dynamic duo padded around in darkness for a while and finally emerged from the orchestra pit to a surprise revelation. Casually sitting at a small damask covered table, sipping chilled chardonnay from Napa Valley, were Rosie O'Donnell and Ellen De Generes.

For a while, the atmosphere was rich with silence as both ladies ogled the personal curvature of my partner. Her legs went all the way up to her armpits. I stepped in front of Maria and addressed O'Donnell. "You dirty fat bitch," I screamed. It was as if I had pushed the magic button. Somebody stepped out from behind a curtain, a gaffer shimmied down one of the stage ropes and people ran down aisles and stepped over seats. They were lawyers, architects, porn stars and even a television weatherman. This was the Grand Alliance of Young Sophisticates. De Generes seemed to be their spokesperson.

"Well, well, well! If it isn't the fuzz. Make yourself comfortable, folks. The show doesn't start until I press the button. Capiche!"

I don't think that the comedienne was comfortable doing Italian jokes but I wasn't worried as there would be no detonation while the gang was all there.

It looked like they were prepared to talk and although I did have negotiating skills, I wasn't even an American so my concessions would amount to zip. I shifted my passport to a deeper pocket and tried to sort this whole mess out. They had already named their new country *Pride* and I accepted this without prejudice. Perhaps I went beyond my authority when I said that we would forget Chula Vista. After all, everybody else already had.

The President even became conciliatory, after he was alerted to the fact that many of the lads and lasses were Democrats. It looked like the administration was going to soften their stance on their gender issues. When I departed the theater, they were talking about moving the Klu Klux Klan out of Mississippi and moving the gays in. They were going to rename the river Ms Sippi.

As the lady with the long legs and I walked, hand in hand, along West 48th Street, the bright lights of Broadway flickered on. The world was full of light, once again and I asked Maria Bernardo if she would like to come back to Australia with me. She looked at me with those doe eyes of hers. "Sorry, Patrick. I like to be in America." What could I say? As we approached the Schubert Theater, I saw that the box office was doing good business: a tribute to Leonard Bernstein, no less. I purchased two tickets and we went in.

Pest to the rescue.

THE LUNATIC FROM LAREDO

This was not the first time I had been to the streets of Laredo. I can remember being wrapped in a white sheet and listening to Johnny Cash's version of that famous dirge. Until I was twelve years of age, I always went to bed dreaming of cowboys. Then I discovered *Playboy* magazine.

Paddy Pest arrived in Laredo by *Greyhound* bus. One chooses this kind of transportation in order to avoid the scrutiny of those airport metal detectors. My *Glock* 9x19 caliber automatic is close to my heart and I never like to leave home without it. In fact, I had to suppress an urgent desire to let off a few rounds at the bambino at the back of the bus. The cry baby hadn't let up since we left San Antonio.

We arrived at El Metro terminus early on Sunday morning. The church bells were tolling and all roads led to San Agustin Cathedral. At least, Convent Street and Santa Maria Avenue did. I crossed myself and headed for a nearby diner. They were doing breakfast and the service was quick.

You wouldn't say that the waitress was young; nor would you say that she was thin. However, that was definitely an unfiltered cigarette hanging from her lip. My God! It was eight o'clock in the morning. I accepted her offer of coffee and ordered a tequila chaser. I knew it was going to be that kind of a day.

I don't often drink alcohol before lunch but I had a lot of thinking to do. My ten thirty appointment would be a delicate confrontation. The client, Angelo Alvarez, was a mover and shaker of the highest order but his reputation as a weasel and slime-bag had not gone un-noticed by my due-diligence process. However, the receipt of an advance payment torpedoed any rational thoughts of caution that should have been apparent. I just had to accept that he was a worm and hope that I could complete my mission before somebody put him where he belonged. They always have a Boot Hill in these kinds of towns.

"Mr Paddy Pest! What a great pleasure. I have heard so much about the suave and sophisticated crime fighter from Australia. Welcome to Laredo."

Angelo's hand-shake was strong and he flashed a smile that would win first prize at a dentist's convention. There were two bodyguards in attendance and he dismissed them contemptuously. A cigar was offered and refused. I knew that he was sizing me up and I wondered what he knew about me apart from the fact that I was cheap. There had obviously been some kind of recommendation but it could have come from someone who wanted me dead: waiters and ex-girlfriends, mainly.

You may be aware that Laredo sits comfortably on the Rio Grande and is a popular entrance point into Mexico. What comes out of Mexico is even more substantial and I was quick to assure Angelo that I had no truck with drugs. He told me not to get so excited and gave me a Valium. He also stated that they didn't use trucks.

The morning meeting dragged on and soon it was time for chow. We retired to a nearby cantina for lunch. It was his treat and he wouldn't let me leave without sampling most of the dishes, each a little hotter than the last. What could I do but try and douse the fire with copious quantities of their local brew? By four o'clock, he was my dearest buddy and I was prepared to do anything for a friend. Some hours later, his bodyguards deposited my incoherent carcass in my motel room and turned out the lights. What sweet guys!

I awoke with a blinding hangover but was pleased to find a packet of Nurofen on the side table next to a thin manila folder that I had never seen before. Don't tell me that I had committed to whacking somebody. Paddy Pest doesn't do that kind of thing.

Sure enough, the file contained one photograph, which was clipped to a condolence card. The name, Mayor Beauregard Didi Lee was not familiar to me. I suppose they called him Bo Diddley for short. The picture had been taken at a function and the smiling mayor was surrounded by a group that may well have been his inner circle of friends and contemporaries. The severe-looking lady to his immediate left could not have been more conspicuous if she were wearing a pork-pie hat in a synagogue. She was dressed as a nurse. In fact, one would have to assume that she was a nurse. The forty-something battle-axe carried one of those medical fob watches and there was a thermometer in her top pocket. I have often fantasized about having a private nurse but you would have to think that, when this lady had been pressed into service, the mayor wasn't making his own decisions.

I immediately headed for the city's main library in order to access public records. Mayor Lee was already a conundrum and I was interested in learning more about his history and his health. I was also keen to determine what he had done to piss-off Angelo Alvarez.

"Excuse me, Ma'am. Could you direct me to the section for confidential records and unsubstantiated rumors?"

Beau Didier Lee had a Chinese/French background and had drifted into Texas from New Orleans some years ago. He had been a restaurateur and remained so, even after he decided to enter the political arena. Alvarez was also in the hospitality business but concentrated on low-life bars and brothels. You have to understand that standards are not high in this city. The most popular bar in town is called Average Joe's. Alvarez also ran a bus company that did not advertise its routes in and out of Mexico. His buses were the only ones that were fitted with pontoons to help them cross the Rio Grande.

Although there was no obvious animosity between the two king-pins of Laredo society, I could see why Angelo would be less than impressed with Beau's track record. After a short period in office, the mayor had closed five illegal brothels, initiated arrest warrants on half-a-dozen prominent citizens for corruption and introduced a crippling tax on all non-government amphibious vehicles. The strange thing about these public records was that there was no personal information in relation to Mr Lee except for the fact that he was a member of the congregation at Our Lady of Guadalupe Catholic Church. As was Angelo Alvarez!

I decided to put a tail on Beauregard Lee. This wasn't difficult as his official functions were publicized. His night time excursions were of more interest to me and so I eased in behind the Mayormobile as it departed City Hall at the end of the day. His eventual destination surprised me – the Graylands Mental Institution. The word was out that this place was haunted. I could believe that and had no desire to move any closer than the leafy sycamore tree near the main gate. With my high-powered binoculars,

I spied the mayor and his nurse alighting from the vehicle, which sped off through the gate. Perhaps to return, later!

Did I nod off? Of course I did. Only to wake with the birds when I heard the vehicle return. Good grief! The man had spent the night at the funny farm.

The results of another day's surveillance were not so illuminating and quite predictable: the opening of a senior's accommodation facility; lunch with a concerned citizens group and finally, he had to judge a tamale-eating contest. Throughout the day his nurse hardly left his side and I saw no pills being dispensed. I had presumed that this was her function. I was relieved when the big vehicle once again left City Hall with me in hot pursuit. This time, there were a few stops: the video store and *The China Bo Restaurant* for some take-out. I wondered whether he was a silent partner in the enterprise. His final destination was the same as the previous evening and the vehicle departed the scene as before. Then it dawned on me. The mayor of Laredo actually lived at the asylum. He was a nutter. I was absolutely stunned.

As I tried to digest the enormity of this revelation, I thought I saw a long black limousine slide by. Was that one of Angelo's goons in the front seat? I guessed that the big man would be getting a bit impatient for some action but I am sure that they would have been impressed with my dedicated stakeout; or else they were waiting to pop me once I had disposed of Mr Lee.

In all honesty, I was never comfortable with this job and now that I had learned that the proposed victim was a hapless crazy person, my enthusiasm waned considerably. I would have no hesitation in providing Angelo Alvarez with his just desserts and this prospect was a distinct possibly. After all, I was pretty sure that I was to be treated with extreme prejudice, whatever the outcome. My part-time secretary and dolly-girl, Dolores, had already been on the blower to advise that Angelo's check had bounced.

"Paddy, the bank says that there is no such organization as Integrity Trust Inc. I hope you didn't have to pay for lunch."

It's a sad world that we live in where even crooks can't be trusted. Nevertheless, I put all these thoughts aside as I tried to determine who might be responsible for having the mayor committed to a mental institution. It was time to return to the official records and I did so with relish (there's a hot dog stand outside the library). It soon became apparent that Beau Lee was a mayor like none other before him. He had reduced parking fees, senior citizens were eligible for free travel and he had abolished racial discrimination at the local boat club. No wonder everybody thought he was mad. Especially, when all the boats went missing.

I decided that it would be a good idea to meet the guy and I presented myself as a boat-builder from Australia. I was offered an immediate audience. I tried to be as vague as possible as there has been quite a few famous boat-builders from Australia. One of them, Ben Lexcen, was responsible for winning the America's Cup.

If he had a mental illness, it was not immediately discernable. Although she didn't take part in the conversation, Nurse Grimsby remained in the room and glared at me with undisguised contempt. Although my conversational efforts and repartee found their mark with the mayor, the medical misanthrope could only simmer in her sad and sorry world of medication and therapy. I wondered who could have put her up for this job. I decided to test them both out. I mentioned the name Angelo Alvarez.

Well! Tickle my ass with a feather and call me stupid. I couldn't believe what happened next. Lee's face became contorted and turned a vivid shade of purple. His whole body started shaking and Nurse Grimsby ran around the room in a state of perplexity. She was continually screaming "Oh no." It needed both of us to restrain him from jumping out of the window and I sat on his chest while she injected him with a quick-acting relaxant. When it was all over, he casually mopped his brow with his handkerchief and enquired "Angelo who?"

He probably thought that a brainless boat-builder from a dumb-ass country in the middle of no-where would hardly pick-up on his surprise reaction to my question. Little did he know that most of my relatives are psychopaths and I am quick to recognize the signs? In truth, I suspected that he was not fully aware of the extent of his own reaction. After all, he was a loony, wasn't he?

I managed a few moments alone with the nurse and she wasn't a bad sort, once she had undone some of those buttons that had been restraining her inhibitions. There is an art to extracting information from women and Paddy Pest is the best in the business. When I left the building, there was very little that I didn't know about Angelo Alvarez or Nurse Grimsby.

It will not surprise any of you to learn that the nasty nurse from the nut-house was in cahoots with the angelic Mr Alvarez. Mandy Grimsby had been a madam at one of Angelo's entertainment venues when he decided that he needed someone at the sharp end of his empire who knew something about drugs. So, he sponsored her through nursing school and arranged a posting at Graylands Mental Institution. He had not anticipated that there would be a fly in the ointment – Beau Didi Lee.

Bo Diddley swept into power on the back of general dissatisfaction with the incumbent administration. Corruption was rife and there was no-one who was more corrupt than Angelo. The new mayor immediately laid down the law, which was embarrassing for those who were committed to upholding the law. Both the police chief and a senior judge were major players at Angelo's craps tables and were not unknown to Miss Mandy.

Mayor Lee was able to introduce his reforms without resistance because he had a good team around him and they were like a protective ring of fire. Johnny Cash would have been proud. The villains tried everything and even attempted to poison his yum-cha. They detonated a bomb at his home before breakfast and even sent him a long-playing CD of Freddy Fender. However, his brain failed to explode.

Angelo was aware that Beau was quite a devout Christian and attended the church known as Our Lady of Guadalupe. He put Mandy in a nun's outfit and sent her over there as a Pastoral Assistant. The priest needed all the help that he could get. For the next six weeks, Beau Lee took communion from Sister Mandy and nobody noticed that the wafer had been dipped in a slow-acting poison. In reality, Mandy had stuffed up. The poison mix was not right and instead of a fatal dose, Beau was subject to intermittent outbursts, similar to that which I have already described. For some reason, he only reacted to the names Angelo, Benedict or Jesus. It must have been a Catholic thing.

Obviously, there must have been a few people in his group that took the name of the Lord in vain because he produced quite a few outbursts and they decided that he was ready to be committed. However, he was doing such a good job that they didn't want to retire him. A solution presented itself when the central committee heard that Sister Mandy had relinquished her role at Our Lady's church and rejoined the staff at the insane asylum. She was immediately appointed as his private nurse. Need I say that you are now fully acquainted with the situation?

Sometimes, explanations are important and, in other situations, they are of no value. As in this instance! The fact is that I was supposed to kill Mr Lee and then, in all probability, there would be a bullet with my name on it. It made more sense to dispose of my client. There would be no payment in either case but I would have struck a blow for Laredo; not to mention justice and the American way.

I invited Angelo to dinner on the pretext that I was going to explain my plan and give him an opportunity to arrange an alibi. I knew that the bodyguards would hang around out back and get a few morsels from the kitchen staff. Little did they know that they were my kitchen staff?

The thing about Mexican food is that everyone expects to hit the toilet after a few dishes. It doesn't matter whether you are eating tacos, tortillas, enchiladas or hot tamales. My guys had laced the food with the necessary encouragement and in a stroke of impeccable timing, Angelo and his two cronies arrived at the caballero wash-room at roughly the same time. I don't know who pushed the flush button first because I had wired all three cubicles. The back half of the restaurant exploded with such force, I feared that there might be collateral damage but there wasn't.

"Gee, Paddy. If they find out that you are responsible, there will be an almighty stink."

"There is already an almighty stink. Let's get out of here, Dolores."

We stayed in town for the funeral and it was a grand affair. Mayor Lee delivered the eulogy and the three bodies were displayed, wrapped in white linen. For a change, they played the Marty Robbins version of *Cowboy's Lament (The Streets of Laredo)* and I couldn't help whistling along.

Mandy Grimsby was nowhere to be seen but I suspect that she was tied up somewhere with one of her clients.

Footnote: *The Streets of Laredo* is one of the most recorded songs in the *Country and Western* genre. The Don Edwards version on *YouTube* offers a backdrop of archival images sourced from the town library, including Laredo City Hall. There are no surviving pictures of Mayor Beau Lee (if, in fact, any ever existed).

–2–

THE ACHIEVERS

Pamela	56	Hakim	80
Halle	66	Bronnie	90
Dick	73	Tyrone	97

In my last book, I provided my readers with an insight into the lifestyles of my friends and acquaintances. These people bear no resemblance to the riff-raff that feed off that scoundrel Paddy Pest.

They were mostly average urbanites with boring jobs and a predictable existence. A lot like you, I expect. Yet, there are so many people out there whose lives can be an inspiration to us all and I know many of them. Well, I would, wouldn't I?

I don't want you to be jealous of these high fliers. Their level of achievement is no more than you can attain, if you have the right attitude. It is a long way to the top and, often, it can take quite some time to get there. There is no short cut to fame and fortune.

Well, perhaps there is. Why don't you just go out and buy a lottery ticket.

PAMELA

Pam awoke one morning and decided that she wanted to become prime minister.

"Really Pamela, you must be dreaming," said her bemused mother. "I don't know where you get this driving ambition from. Certainly, not your father."

The youngster was in her first year at university and was an enthusiastic member of the student union. Being a member of such a group was often a clever way to meet somebody exciting from the opposite sex. In fact, Pam was totally infatuated with Johnny Baker, a very smart student with the bluest eyes she had ever seen. He was a member of the Labor Club, so she also applied for membership.

"Do you, Pamela Raylene Gilhooley, swear by almighty God that you will be faithful and bear true allegiance to the Labor Club and to pay your statutory fees when they fall due?"

With a sweet smile, she condescendingly replied. "I do."

Unfortunately, Johnny Baker, the object of her affection, was besotted with Natalie Baumgartner, who had big knockers. Pamela's twelve-year-old brother, Stanley, was unusually sympathetic when he heard of her heartbreak and his statement of regret was tinged with overtones of knowledgeable insight that is often found amongst those who have been similarly rejected.

"Gee, Sis. What bad luck?"

Rather than become despondent, Pamela immersed herself in the politics of the Labor Club and quickly secured a reputation for being a radical firebrand. Perception was everything and her flaming red hair contributed to her mystique, especially at various campus rallies, which were no place for the faint-hearted. The opposing factions often out-numbered the converted and fisticuffs and brawling were the order of the day. Flying objects such as soft-drink bottles, beer cans and flour bombs were acceptable missiles. Everybody had a great time except for the people who had to clean everything up.

Pamela's parents were pacifists and were beside themselves when she would arrive home, bedraggled and bleeding. Where did they go wrong? Her long-suffering teacher, Brooke Winterbottom, remembers the young girl fighting all the way from kindergarten to high school.

"I seem to recall that when Simon Shannon put his hand up her dress during her fifth birthday party in the playroom, she kneed him in the groin and stomped on him. It was very ugly."

Over the years, she honed her skills in this area and was a potent force whenever the constabulary arrived to quell dissent that was tediously repetitive at most student protests. One such demonstration erupted on campus just prior to a particularly spiteful general election. The hot issue was the plight of asylum seekers. Both sides of the argument had persuaded high profile celebrities to take part in an outdoor debate. Pamela had won early plaudits from the Labor Party by recruiting one of the Catholic Church's leading luminaries. Bishop Anderson was rarely out of the limelight and attracted a large following. However, there were detractors.

He had an annoying habit of speaking with his hands and his overbearing gestures fueled scorn and derision from some. They called him Hands Christian Anderson.

Across the table, things could not have been more confrontational. Senator Buck Wilson was such a red neck he would not have been out of place at a Turkey Shoot. He was impolite, aggressive, profane and unyielding. The fact that he was also cynically agnostic and irreverent did not reduce the tension between the two lead speakers.

"I'll personally escort each and every one of these illegal immigrants back to where they come from. God help me." Spluttered the Senator.

"Spoken like a true agnostic," replied the smug and smarmy bishop."

Ten minutes into the debate, they witnessed the first flare. This seemed to spark anarchy as the quadrangle erupted into chaos and mass hysteria. Nothing seemed to be on fire but there was a lot of smoke about. The bells of the fire engines possibly exacerbated the situation.

Less than a dozen students ended up in the watch-house, that night, which is about par for this kind of insurrection. Pam was one of them. She had been intercepted on her way to the clock-tower: dragging a significant banner that proclaimed that Mother Teresa loved asylum seekers. Of course, Mother Teresa had been dead for some years but the bishop had indicated that she was still on top of things. Unfortunately, she would not be on top of the clock-tower.

Ray Gilhooley had bailed out his daughter so many times that the police had given him his own parking space. He was hardly convinced by her assertions that this periodic detention was valuable work experience for someone who was going to become a lawyer. However, he resisted comment in case he received the pursed lips and disdainful stare that only Pamela could deliver with such chilling contempt. He was more worried by the increasing number of male visitors who attended Pam's room for the weekly meeting of the Chocolate Lover's Society, another one of her union activities. Someone was messing with his daughter and he wasn't pleased.

One of those teenage despoilers was someone who proudly carried the sobriquet of Decadent Daryl. He was chuffed to think that he might be compared to Bacchus, Caligula or Nero and, thus, the chocolate club was an obvious fit for him. It is difficult to understand why Pamela fancied

Daryl's chocolates but she did. The decadent one was invited to all the best parties and Pam couldn't get this kind of a rush from the dreary socialists who provided the only alternative.

Many of these social outings took place in the elite suburbs and glamorous beach houses of the rich and famous, where a university degree was accepted as a natural extension of a private school education. One couldn't help but think that this was better work experience than a night in the jug. After all, these people couldn't have made all their money without help from a good lawyer. In truth, most of these people were good lawyers.

To her credit, she was never tempted to deny her working-class roots and privately promised herself that she would never succumb to easy money. I might remind you that she was still a little immature, unrealistically optimistic and hopelessly naïve. Nevertheless, she did what had to be done. She dumped Daryl and took out a membership with a Western District football club. Now all she had to do was find someone who could explain the rules to her.

Lisping Les LeVingt was the official masseur for the girls' softball club, the netball team and the women's chess club and was an authority on all things football. He was fond of Pam and they stayed in contact, even when it was discovered that he wasn't really a student of the university or anywhere else. Nobody had ever asked to see his credentials. They would have discovered that he was a storeman and packer and his union dues were fully paid up.

If you want to be a serious politician in Australia, you just have to know your sport and Pam absorbed everything in great detail, including the long-term effects of a knee reconstruction or the dreaded osteitis pubis. She couldn't have had a better teacher for that one. Lisping Les had made himself an authority on groins, although most of them were female. They attended home games together and she even fraternized with the team. In fact, she was once discovered in a hot tub with half of the forward line and the club mascot (a four-year-old Bull terrier).

I expect that this was a liberating experience but not so much as the day she moved out of home and into digs with two of her fellow students.

"Mom, Pop! It's over. I'm moving out. I'm going to become a liberated woman."

Her mother curbed her natural disappointment and put on a brave front.

"That's nice, dear. I expect that you'll still be back for pot roast on Monday and bingo on the week-end." Pam thought about the bingo for all of ten seconds. "Maybe the pot roast. Say good-bye to Stanley for me." And she was gone. Just like that.

Beth and Candice were both old school anarchists and feminists to boot. They gave Pam the room along the corridor that was splashed with disparaging slogans from feminist icons such as Germaine Greer, Gloria Steinem, Virginia Woolf and Wonder Woman. A male visitor would never tread this path without some confidence that satisfaction would be the ultimate reward and it usually was.

Not all of these young studs were students or footballers. Vince was the barker at his father's fruit stall at the Victoria Market and he always insisted on providing home delivery. She could never get rid of him, not that she tried that hard. The romance did not last and neither did Vince Valenti. It turned out that he was a mole for the Victoria Police.

One day he didn't turn up for work and was never seen again. A distressed relative confided to Pamela that he was with the fishes. This quaint expression originates from southern Italy and defines an out-of-favor associate who is trying to dog-paddle while wearing concrete boots. I may have mentioned earlier that Pam was a little naïve. She went looking for him at the fish market and, as luck would have it, her timing was exquisite. The market was closing and they had reduced the price of green prawns by half. The girls were in for a treat that night.

The next boy-friend to appear on the scene carried the nick-name *The Stool Pigeon*. Dr Lindsay Bird was a young urologist from one of the teaching hospitals and, although there was an age difference, they seemed to click for a while. The girls were amused that Pam had hooked up with someone else who was an authority on body-parts to be found below the belt. Yes, Lisping Les was still very much on the scene, although his credits were somewhat devalued after a number of complaints had been received concerning his massaging techniques.

As a storeman and packer, the man in question was in an enviable position to help the girls equip their sparsely decorated house and his ability to acquire certain goods at less than wholesale price was impressive. The flame-haired student was in her third year and would soon have to think about career options: a criminal lawyer or industrial advocate. Either way, she would probably have the same clients and all of them would be known to Les.

You have to have a certain charisma and understanding when dealing with clientele who are in trouble. As often as not, you are the referral of last resort and those who have gone before have usually messed things up. Two names that keep cropping up are Messrs Smith and Wesson. Boys have always had a fascination with guns. If given the opportunity, most lawyers will suggest arbitration as a means of dispute management but what do they know?

Whereas our heroine did come to grips with her academic responsibilities, it was also a watershed year in terms of her political awakening and a time when she was able to shrug off her righteous schoolgirl indignations and embrace the deep and meaningful struggle of the proletariat. She became a communist.

"Do you, Pamela Raylene Gilhooley, swear by almighty God that you will be faithful and bear true allegiance to the Communist Party and to pay your statutory fees when they fall due?"

With a sweet smile, she condescendingly replied. "I do."

Although Pamela had already been radicalized, there had never been any kind of firm ideological bonding that would signify total commitment. Around this time, Che Guevara was the poster boy for the socialist resistance and his image was redolent with determination and resolve. The artistic corridor of iconic feminists that led to Pam's bedroom had now been replaced with depictions of Marx, Lenin, Castro and other scruffy guys with headbands and beards.

It was a good time to be involved because the issues were real; none more so than the indignation of the Chinese community when they learned that the city was prepared to pay homage to the Dalai Lama. One restaurateur in Chinatown was so aggrieved that he threatened to take off the numbers from his menu. It didn't seem to matter that if the *Gwailos* didn't know what they were ordering they would go elsewhere.

Pam's student union was in a position to help muddy the waters as they often held their revolutionary meetings at cheap eateries like *Yip Doodle Yum Cha*. It was the only restaurant in town that would give you a discount if you were a card-carrying communist. Nevertheless, the place was deceptive. The life-size photo of Yip Doodle in the foyer was more Charlie Chan than Chairman Mao.

This particular dispute did not have Pamela's absolute support. The student strategy was to infiltrate airport security and scatter itching powder down the great man's robes.

"What is he doing arriving in mid-winter dressed like that? Let's inundate his under-pants."

Where is the respect? Normally, Pam would be up for something trite and ludicrous but she actually had a soft spot for the old geezer in the orange outfit. The outrage over the increased price of meat pies in the cafeteria was another matter. Pam always impressed with her advocacy skills and it was through her efforts that the cafeteria dispute was settled. The price increase was reduced by half and although appeasement was obtained, there was some residual bitterness. In an affront to the left-leaning reactionaries, management refused to provide any red-colored sauces as an accompaniment.

Pam had a beautiful speaking voice and her modulated tones of reason always calmed the choppy waters and turned the tide of confrontation. She was also an attractive woman. It was no wonder that people were starting to sit up and take notice.

In the period following her graduation, the articulate advocate fielded solicitations from many randy solicitors and it took all her dexterous ingenuity to keep her briefs were they were. Nevertheless, she needed to be flexible. After all, one doesn't want to offend any possible professional mentor.

Being able to use people in a manipulative manner can be a positive advantage if your vocation in life is political or business orientated. Our girl had quickly shed her mantle of innocence and blossomed into a feisty litigator who was not to be taken lightly. In her first class action against a callous and malevolent multi-national, Pam represented the rights of the little people like never before.

"Dwarf-throwing is an insidious business, Your Honor. These people have exceeded the social boundaries in the avaricious pursuit of a fast buck." The judge peered down at the slip of a girl. "Thank you, young lady. I believe that I just asked you for your name."

Soon, everybody would know her name. Pamela prevailed with a glorious victory that put her on the front pages of all the dailies.

Many saw the larrikin lawyer as a future political asset, so she was nominated for selection at a branch meeting of the local Labor Party and was subsequently elected. I think that those prime ministerial ambitions resurfaced within seconds of her maiden speech in the parliament. Everybody said that it was a cracking oratory and there was even talk that she may replace a non-performing liability in the outer cabinet.

This didn't happen, mainly due to a bad experience with a state-of-the-art animal shelter that she had been promoting. They had built the place slap-bang up against the rear of the largest Chinese restaurant in her electorate. Somebody noticed that animals were systematically vanishing from their cages. It was discovered that they were disappearing into the bowels of the Chung Palace and re-appearing as a protein supplement in Dim Sims and other take-out tidbits.

Pamela was a forward thinker and she wasn't going to let these small blemishes interfere with the big picture. The secret was to promote yourself while, simultaneously, undermining the prospects of any competitor. This had to be done in an unobtrusive manner and without any possibility of personal repercussions.

In a bad period for the government, one of the party's most admired policy-makers was outed as a pedophile and forced to resign in a blaze of publicity. The heir apparent was also nobbled before he could step into the breach: an immigration scandal. This left Pamela Gilhooley as the obvious replacement. She graciously accepted the challenge amidst informed rumor that she was responsible for the leaks that sabotaged two promising careers. Their humiliation was complete when they had to listen to her cabinet room soliloquy of solace before they were escorted from the building.

Pam was elated to be finally acknowledged and she prospered in her new role. As the years rolled by, the lady became a confident politico of undoubted ability. There were few people in the party who didn't agree that she was the person most likely but none of them were prepared for what happened next.

The party's much-loved leader had traveled to Queensland to officially launch the country's first home-grown detention center for asylum seekers who were waiting for residency consideration. It was a massive project that covered a large area and the developers were there with all their equipment, just waiting for the Prime Minister to cut the ribbon and turn the first sod.

In a major administrative blunder, the bureaucrats had failed to notice that the construction site was a traditional burial place of the once-feared Ankamuti people, an indigenous tribe renowned for their pride and inflexibility. The Prime Minister, who was a bit of a silver tongue, agreed to a coffee stop with the elders on the way to the ceremonial opening. He believed that if he couldn't calm the waters, the worst case scenario would surely be the American option.

"We can build them a casino in the desert with a graveyard attached."

However, the coffee break did not go well. The elders arrived with the whole tribe and they were a recalcitrant bunch. The waters were not calmed and eyebrows were raised when their spiritual leader ordered a flat white. He usually had cocoa and a muffin. Later in the day, the security services determined that this had been an Aboriginal Jihad call, to be acted upon by anyone with balls and a steely determination.

To cut a long story short, the PM severed the ribbon and the equipment operators leapt into action. It was unfortunate that the silver-tongued devil dallied in order to chat-up a couple of Gold Coast meter-maids, who were there to supervise the parking. Somebody pushed him in front of a steam-roller and the giant vehicle could not stop.

The Prime Minister's flat remains were buried in the family plot and the funeral was televised nationwide. The cabinet meeting to elect a replacement PM was a somber affair and there was no mood for any decision other than the obvious. Pam was the runaway victor and in her most articulate manner, she waxed lyrical about her commitment to the

Australian people and her belief in justice for all. In a reflective mood, she mused about her long journey to the top which all seemed far removed from that student awakening, all those years ago.

Perhaps dreams do come true.

HALLE

Many of you will be shocked to learn that Halle and I are no longer an item. That's all there is to it, really. You know how it goes. You drift apart and all of a sudden you are both bored beyond belief. She was not the first James Bond cup-cake that I have been involved with and it is not easy to live up to expectations. I am suave and charismatic in my own right and also an expert on Fabergé eggs and vintage port. But it is never enough.

Halle and I got together in strange circumstances. We were on the set of her Bond movie and I was providing technical advice. What some people don't know is that sometimes I can be a bit of a klutz and my attention span is not what it should be. In short, I walked into the ladies toilet by mistake and found her there: stark naked. She was playing a CIA agent in the film and few people realized that we had our own little joke. She later told people that I called her CIA because it meant *caught in the altogether*.

The odds were never short concerning the longevity of the relationship, as I was a bit of a cad.

"He's a bid of a cad, Halle. Just keep him away from those Miss World contestants." This from people who didn't know that she was a Miss World contestant, herself.

Sure, I had a bit of a roving eye and there will be women out there who are reading this piece and will want to have my guts for garters, if not another part of my anatomy. The truth is that I understand and sympathize with their views. If it wasn't for the fact that I am a dyed-in-the-wool male chauvinistic pig, I would be a very real supporter of affirmative action.

I just want you to know that Halle had not only been a contestant in this particular pageant but also many others as well. At one stage, she was named the sexiest person alive.

It is probably difficult for many of you to picture me with the sexiest woman alive and that is why I have included a gratuitous photo of our day at Santa Monica. I wasn't cut out to be gawked at but she was used to it, so that wasn't the reason that she looks so unhappy. I had just refused to buy her a paddle pop and, quite frankly, I was uninterested in her pleading and begging. Barbara Broccoli, the producer of the Bond films, wanted her to look her best and I helped out by playing Gestapo Man, when she tried to circumvent her diet with tasty treats.

Normally, I am a person of understanding and compassion with a heart of gold. You may recall that when Jinx Johnson was putting it all on the line for her country, her journey took her to Iceland, where there was quite a bit of frost about. In fact, until Mr Bond came along, the heroine was in more trouble than a Hershey bar at a grizzly bear's picnic. Breaking out from that ice prison was difficult to film and there were many takes. Understandably, she caught a severe chill and of all the sympathetic fellows who volunteered to spread some vapor rub on her chest, she chose me.

I suspect that she saw me as some kind of kindred spirit as I used to cough a bit, also. People's addictions and allergies vary from the dangerous to the ridiculous. I represent one of the latter. I am allergic to chocolate. When I told Halle about this, after our first intimate moment, she laughed. "Hey lover, did anyone ever tell you that you need glasses?"

As you might know, Halle's mom was Caucasian and her father was

African-American but the one who had the greatest identity crisis was her sister, who was Swiss. Well, I think she was. After all, her name is Heidi. They don't talk much these days but in your hour of need, you always find shelter in the bosom of your family. When their girl won a Razzie (Golden Raspberry Award) for her role as Catwoman, they knew that an emotional earthquake was about to erupt.

Who would have thought? A worst acting award only a few years after her Oscar for Monster's Ball! Everyone was shocked that she intended to collect the award in person, which she did: to my mind, a very brave and fearless initiative. I felt extremely spineless with my decision to dump her in the aftermath of the announcement. Fortunately, I recanted before she got a whiff of my intentions. After all, there had already been one unexpected exodus and she was in a fragile state. Her favorite moggy had left home in disgust, never to return.

What is it with women and the animals that they live with? I am talking about the four-legged variety that they feed, nurture, indulge and pamper in an obvious attempt to elicit unconditional loyalty from them. This is something that you can't always get from husbands and lovers and, to tell you the truth, I would have thought that cats were a debatable asset. Why don't you test them without a can of tuna in your hand?

Around this time, there was a rumor that Halle kept the Bengal tiger from the Catwoman movie as a pet but this was not true. Having co-star, Sharon Stone and a Bengal tiger on the same movie set must have been a challenge. If they ever came to blows, I don't think that the smart money would be on the tiger. Nevertheless, it appears that the two super-stars hit it off. I am not sure whether this is just show-business speak or they actually liked each other. In a rather strange prelude to their pairing, Halle had played a character called Sharon Stone in the movie, *The Flintstones*, some ten years earlier.

If you were wondering what I was doing ten years earlier, I can tell you. Once again, we are looking at six degrees of separation. I mentioned earlier that her ladyship wasn't the first Bond girl that I had messed with and I know that most of you will immediately presume that it was Pussy Galore. You would be wrong. Those of you who have read my previous book would remember that I had a tempestuous four-day marriage to

Honey Ryder, who mesmerized Bond when she emerged from the briny in an eye-catching bikini that also caught the eye of the despicable Dr No. Was it a coincidence that the technical advisor for *Die Another Day* determined that Jinx Johnson should emerge in similar gear to catch 007's eye? What a sleaze he was (Bond, not me).

Whereas Halle is quite fetching in a bikini, I am not at my most alluring when wearing budgie smugglers and other forms of swim wear. Certainly, I am suave and I do have a magnetic personality but my physical dimensions are not what you would expect to see on the red carpet, escorting a stunning piece of crumpet like Halle. Some people have even been rude enough to suggest that I would be more comfortable with her aunt, Juniper Berry. This snide remark refers to my penchant for the occasional gin sling, which keeps me going when my book sales are down, which is mostly always.

"Darling, do have another gin and stop worrying about those book sales. We can always use them for door-stops or something."

My therapist has told me that good-looking chicks are sometimes prepared to ignore your physical imperfections, if you are a writer. Marilyn Monroe set these wheels in motion when she hooked up with Arthur Miller, who looked like death warmed up. I must admit that I missed the Shrek movies and I often wondered whether he was, in fact, a writer. We actually have a lot in common with ogres, especially if working as a critic.

As I move on in pursuit of a younger companion, I always like to look back on the previous liaison and see if I can determine whether things could have been better. On reflection, I regret that I tried to kill Halle. I think that this attempted homicide soured our relationship to some extent. Eventually, we patched things up but it was never the same. Especially with her bosom buddy, Sharon Stone, still on the scene.

"I don't trust that bastard. Here, put this ice pick under your pillow."

The years are starting to roll by a little faster than they used to and I worry for the pretty little model, beauty queen and actor. Hollywood doesn't treat forty-something women very well and with every additional wrinkle or blemish, her star is likely to wane. Although you don't need ten million big ones (per movie) to keep yourself in nail polish, the pecking order is important, especially in a town where ego is everything.

Some people have said that I also have a bit of an ego but I think that I am actually shy, reserved and conservative. How I wish I had the chutzpah that young people possess. They see an opportunity and they take it. No false remorse or shame! The other day, I was down by the lake, taking a few of my masterful photos, when a sixteen or seventeen year old lass appeared from no-where. I suspect that she was on her way home from school.

"Would you like to feel my tits for twenty bucks?"

Now, you will have to take my word for it that this was very good value but I was my usual reticent self. After all, in America, twenty dollars is never twenty dollars. You have to add on tax and then there is the tip on top of that. If you underpay the gratuity, you will know it immediately.

"Have a nice day, you jerk."

I don't think that Halle spent much time down by the lake but those early years must have been pretty competitive in Ohio. Her first beauty crown was Miss Teen All American and the following year she was runner-up in the Miss USA pageant. This kind of thing makes people sit up and take notice and I know that some pretty big producers started dusting off their casting couches as soon as they saw her.

The perception of the Hollywood producer is that he is overweight, overbearing and over indulgent. What can I say? They take chances and are rewarded handsomely if they are successful. Their address books are the envy of all and if they smoke big Cuban cigars, it is probably because they have a personal relationship with Fidel Castro.

Ms Berry's agent smoked foul-smelling stogies that he purchased from a kiosk on Sunset Boulevard every Friday. He then made his studio rounds with his portfolio of aspiring actresses. As often as not, the producer would choose one in order to get him out of the office as quickly as possible and that is how Halle got her start; not that she didn't surprise and delight because she did.

This dazzling beauty quickly became a dedicated professional, borne out by the fact that Halle not only picked up an Oscar but a Golden Globe, an Emmy and a little something from the Screen Actors Guild. Sometimes it can be a curse being a great beauty because people don't take you seriously. On top of that, there is sometimes significant sexual harassment from your co-stars, the director, the cameraman or the leading lady's personal masseur. This is a non-paying job but you have to start out in Juarez, Mexico. That is where the application queue presently ends.

I can empathize with someone in this position because they paid me squat for being a technical advisor on *Die Another Day*. In fact, the doorman at the sound studio refused to believe that I worked there at all, even after I gave him my best Sean Connery impersonation. Didn't I tell you that I was a klutz? I had forgotten that Pierce Brosnan now had the role. Fortunately, Halle came by and was taken by my rakish Australian charm and I managed to be swept onto the set in the backwash of her petticoat.

It didn't take Pierce long to recognize that we were cut from the same cloth. His first wife was Australian and my first father was Irish. I was educated in a Catholic institution and so was he, so both of us understand that you can have two fathers.

The erudite people who purchased my first two books will be aware of my standing within the intelligence community. It is an impressive resume and although many will question the number of unsubstantiated reports that were promulgated, the depth of experience is there for all to see. Teaching Brosnan how to do a wheelie on ice in an Aston Martin was a doddle. The sex scenes were more difficult. Halle was OK. She had already produced a real sizzler with Billy Bob in Monster's Ball. However, as I have just told you, Pierce was raised by the Christian Brothers and if they knew how to do that kind of thing, they weren't telling anyone. In the end, everyone muddled through and we used all that left-over ice for our wrap-party. The martini cocktails were shaken not stirred.

Discerning cinema patrons will not be disappointed that I have yet to make any reference to Halle's participation in the X Men franchise, which starred another Australian, Hugh Jackman. Hugh is all right, I suppose, if you like that kind of thing. He acts, sings and dances a bit and is an all round nice guy. However, that Wolverine character is not a good look. I must say that I am always a little confused with werewolves and vampires. Does he sleep in a coffin or what?

I know this chap who is a bit of an expert with thoroughbred horses and he always says that when you come to the end, there's always a tale and this is so in Halle's case. After we ended our relationship, she blossomed beyond belief. There was a child, her contract was renewed with Revlon and she produced a knock-out portrayal of Dorothy Dandridge for HBO.

I leave you my memories of a lovely lady who will embrace posterity by virtue of her film credits, an Academy Award and this motley paperback, which, I am assured, is rat-proof but prone to volume discounting. If there is some kind of moral to this story, it might be that there is a brown-eyed girl for you out there somewhere. If the only bond you have with your current partner is her apron strings, it may be time to move on.

It's not always easy being a cad but it can be a whole lot of fun.

DICK

Richard Putney had just discovered that he was a virgin. In the twelve years that he had been on this planet, he had never contemplated having congress with a member of the opposite sex. It was only recently that he had condescendingly included them in his conversations. Now, things were moving along but it was unfortunate that the only advice that he could get on the matter was via his best buddy, Pimples McShane. Unfortunately, this information was second-hand, as it had come from the lad's elder brother, who was reputed to have bonked the town bike in the beer garden of The King's Arms on a cold Saturday night in December.

I shudder to think what it would be like to be cradled in the arms of Michael *Mad Dog* McShane. To his friends he was Mick and he was very catholic in his attitude towards his fellow man. If you displeased him, he would punch, kick or head-butt you, depending on which action would have the greatest shock value. He had acquired his definitive title *Mad Dog* when he kidnapped the neighbor's Dachshund and tried to sell the animal to the local butcher.

"I'm sorry, young man. I know that they are called sausage dogs but we only buy retail."

Irrespective of the advice that he was getting, Richard was aware that the prospect of his sexual awakening any time soon was grim, due to the tight restraints imposed on him by his legal guardians. When you are twelve years of age, it is often difficult to get free time away from your parents. You also have to co-ordinate with your co-conspirator. Little Dick had already penciled-in Samantha Seagrass as the girl most likely.

Sam was a good scout and, in fact, an outstanding member of the district's Girl Guide troop. As you might expect, she was most diligent in upholding the traditions of the Brownies and was prepared for anything – well, except for the Richard Putney charm offensive. Although initially taken back, she managed to rebuff his advances but left the door open for future experimentation. It would be a further three years before his sexual fulfillment would be realized and this wasn't such a bad thing because there were other challenges to be embraced.

Unfortunately, his desire to grow a beard ended in failure but this didn't stop him from investigating other possible outlets for his talent. Quite often, after school, he would meander down to the village coffee shop, where his father was the chief barista. The locals would congregate like displaced émigrés and the world and its problems were discussed in great detail. If you wanted a short macchiato, little Dick would bring it to you and then seat himself on one of the spare chairs that was always available. He thought that he was in the company of real experts and so did they. Their confidence rubbed off on the little fellow and that is why he always believed in himself and his convictions. Perhaps if he had known about some of their convictions, he may not have been so self-assured.

It is true that during his teenage years he went bankrupt four times but this was good experience because he was a quick learner. The guys around the coffee table were full of ideas but they never did anything. They were all tongue and tattoos: two of them were from New Zealand.

During these years, Dick was often seen around the markets that proliferated around the city and soon became a bit of trend-setter in the rag trade. His advisor and sometime girl-friend, Dawn Morningstar, was a daughter of someone in the U.S. Embassy and was studying design at the London College of Fashion. She was able to keep him up-to-date with all the latest American trends and this is how he became involved with edible undies.

Little Richard had developed both physically and mentally and I think that it is appropriate to now call him Big Dick. Certainly, that's what all the girls in Soho were calling him. He was the type of person who would not sign off on a project until he had fully researched it, which is what he did with edible undies. Nevertheless, these kinds of fads don't last long and you have to milk them for all they are worth, as quickly as you can. He did just that and even took them across the water to France, where he knew that they eat anything.

I don't know how many millions he made out of this venture but he certainly prospered. It wasn't long before he was extending his range and introducing new flavors like banana, pear, pineapple, custard and seagrass, in memory of the girl who had liberated him from his virginity. His trips to the Continent opened up a new world. He decided to pull stumps and move to a warmer climate. It wasn't that he didn't like living in England. In fact, he even purchased an island, which was just like home, except for the absence of continued precipitation and an unimaginative tax system.

One lazy afternoon, while sipping a mango daiquiri on the verandah of his ostentatious mansion, he conjured up another fabulous idea that would considerably add to his already sizeable fortune. It was all so simple: a home away from home.

Dick had been to Benidorm in Spain and saw that the Brits liked to have all their home comforts with them when they were on holidays: full English breakfast, warm beer, football telecasts etc. He decided that he would go into the travel business and do it better. So, he purchased another tropical island and made the necessary changes. Dick built British pubs, a Wimpy bar and a bingo hall, to name a few. He produced a replica of the Blackpool pier on the foreshore and awarded the kebab contract to Nigella Lawson and Charlie Saatchi.

Welcome to paradise.

There was no stopping this human dynamo. A cut-price airline was needed to service the holiday destination and he knew a man who knew a man. They put an aircraft together; literally. *Sun and Leisure Underpriced Travel PLC* was up and running and then, the greatest coup of all. He hired retired page three girls as cabin crew. Slut Airlines was immediately a player.

It turned out to be a good ten years for the Caribbean and a good decade for the Slut franchise. More islands were purchased and more aircraft were put into the skies. Dick was making so much money that he didn't know what to do with it. He got married, of course and this helped to deplete his riches but you can't stop the unstoppable. It was a credit to his generous nature that he turned into a philanthropist and became a patron of so many charitable causes. The Vatican considered making him their first non-catholic saint.

Even the women's lobby was on side, irrespective of his penchant for page three girls. In an effort to ingratiate himself with the Australian public, he opened a home for destitute and abandoned women in Sydney. His first wife, who was more or less abandoned herself, ran the show. Evidently, he stepped out into the garden for an after-dinner cigar and never returned.

The locals liked what he was doing and gave him the green light to operate in their fair country. This was a big deal because Aussies can be very suspicious of whining Poms and you need to be very clever to win them over, especially at a time when the move to secede from the Commonwealth is strong. Back home in the Old Dart, pressure was put on the monarch to make some kind of recognizant gesture, so the Queen made him a Knight of the Garter. This was in recognition of his work with women, Down Under.

The Slut brand was now alive and well and highly visible in over three dozen countries. These companies were pretty well running themselves and no-one would have blamed him if he just retired to his tropical paradise and put his feet up. After all, the Chairman was no longer a young man. But what do these people know? Dick Putney was an adventurer and always looking for one more challenge. He just couldn't stay put in the same place for any amount of time. I think that it was an Irish rocket scientist who said:

"In the aftermath of a challenge, there is only defeat or gratification."

I find it strange that he didn't mention broken ribs and legs, a hernia, a severed finger and severe sun stroke because these were some of the legacies that Richard inherited from some of his hair-brained adventures. I don't intend to bore you with the details. Well, maybe just one because it was the most outrageous stunt of all time. You probably remember it from all the front page publicity: *Big Dick to Journey to the Center of the Earth.*

If you thought that the general public was incredulous, you should have been at the base camp in Sumatra, where the local villagers were religiously beholden to their omnipresent volcano. This part of Indonesia has the largest volcanic activity in the world and to identify any one of these angry mountains as dormant is a brave call. Nevertheless, this is where Dick would make his entry into the unknown depths. There were rumblings but mostly rumblings of dissent rather than geophysical activity. He had it all worked out and nothing or no-one would dissuade him.

"I'm going to parachute into the crater and then play it by ear." That sounded like a plan and nobody had the balls to tell him that he was off his rocker.

Slut Textile Industries had developed a heat-resistant nylon canopy that would give him a three-point landing and the same wax process was coated onto both his skis to help him should he need to abort in a hurry. If the volcano did erupt and spit him out, he could ski down the mountain on the lava flow to relative safety. In the end, the whole thing was a fizzer. He made a perfect landing, alright, into the middle of a massive marijuana plantation. The tribe that was cultivating the weed was actually delighted to see him because they didn't get to town very often. They hadn't seen any strangers since Amelia Earhart flew over their volcano in nineteen thirty-seven.

Dick returned to camp and saw a lot of worried faces. No wonder the villagers were ramping up the volcano talk. They had quite a lucrative business going here and if the Englishman opened his mouth, they could all end up in the slammer. Dick smiled at the village elders and spoke softly into his mobile phone. The guy at the other end of the line was his new-business manager in London.

"Get down to the Patent Office, Freddy. We're going into the pharmaceutical business."

There is nothing that an entrepreneur appreciates more than a clever ruse initiated by another entrepreneur that can be turned to your own advantage. Blackmail is such a dirty word and Richard Putney would never have anything to do with that. He just explained to the elders that, with him as their new partner, there would be international marketing advantages.

He departed the country confident that his new partnership would surely prosper and it did. In a few short years, the Slut Pharmaceutical Company of Indonesia became one of the country's biggest exporters. Unfortunately, the inevitable occurred. The dormant volcano finally blew and the cannabis harvest was strewn over all the villages in the first wave of destruction. Dick sent his condolences and a large reconstruction pledge. Nevertheless, he couldn't help but think that they all died with a smile on their face.

That's about it, really. There's not a lot more that you can say about Sir Richard Putney. Of course, you may have realized that I have neglected to visit any of those well-worn rumors that have been circulating for years and why would I? I am not that kind of a person. Well, maybe I can discuss just one rumor because the tabloids did make a meal of it, didn't they? It was all innuendo and hearsay, as it often is. I don't know how some of those editors can live with themselves.

The allegation was that Dick still slept with his teddy bear. Or was it his teddy boy? Never mind! The fact is that the shit hit the fan. He claimed that the press was morally vindictive and he was supported by three of his ex-wives, who all declared that they had never seen him with anyone called Edward. This was strange because nobody had even asked them that question. Prince Edward was somehow drawn into the drama and he was peeved, to say the least. He had just become engaged. In the end, it all fizzled out like these things do. The daily rag offered apologies all around and Paddington Bear withdrew his legal suit in light of a cash inducement.

It's funny, isn't it, how we all like to chop down tall poppies? I suspect that it is all based on envy and who could disagree in Richard's case. All that money and the birds! I can remember one of his famous safaris in the Punjab. Every evening he instructed the porters to erect a tent and he provided the most fabulous food and entertainment. I was mesmerized by the most beautiful Eurasian belly dancer I had ever seen. She had the Star of India in her navel and although she had to return the sapphire to the men from Securicor, Dick's guests enjoyed ten minutes of exquisite pleasure. The gemstone was nice, too. As he explained:

"Why have these things if you can't share them with your friends?"

As it turned out, he didn't actually own the Star of India. It was on loan from a museum in New York and en route to New Delhi for a season at the Slut Institute of Fine Art. Dick was a great patron of the arts but he also had the common touch and never forgot a friend.

When he heard that *Mad Dog* McShane was doing porridge for a very dubious assault and battery charge, he got the lads from Slut Decorations and Refurbishments to pop over to Brixton and smarten up his cell a bit. They left behind a new state-of-the-art television, fluffy pillows with matching curtains and some books on tropical travel destinations for his post-release consideration. Yes, there was a Slut Airlines discount voucher attached. What a guy!

You can't get away from the fact that Dick Putney has been a revelation to the travel industry. He goes where no man has gone before and in the words of Maxwell Smart: *and loving it.* I have no doubt that one day he will be sipping his mango daiquiri at his country club in the center of the earth or maybe on the moon. For now, this world is his oyster. His only regret is that he should have started his conquests a little earlier but who wants to lose their virginity at twelve?

HAKIM

Hakim Halim Abdul Al-Aleem owned over two dozen camels and not surprisingly, Al-Aleem Logistics was the biggest transport franchise in the whole Sahara region. Not bad for an indolent Bedouin with motivational problems. Hakim lived in a large tent and was served by fourteen wives, who attended to his every need. Not that this was all a bed of roses. The constant chatter of fourteen women drove him a little stir crazy. It didn't matter how big his tent was.

Certainly, the man's world was limited and his influence hardly reached beyond the boundaries of the desert but he was comfortable with the Sahara's degree of predictability. That is until a fast-talking Arab from New York sold him a satellite dish and a high definition television set.

"Mr Hakim, Sir! This will change your world. Just think. Your wives can watch *The Desert Song* and *Lawrence of Arabia*. You can enjoy the

Kardashian girls as they let their hair down. Of course, this is a once-only offer."

The once-only offer was snapped up and true to word, Hakim's world really opened up. He marveled at the delights of Europe and America that he saw on the documentary and sport channels. The avid viewer became a devoted fan of Man U and the Boston Red Sox, possibly because he had never worn socks in his life. Like so many of us, he contracted a severe case of travel bug and acted both swiftly and decisively. The number one son was called to his side and empowered to take over control of Al-Aleem Logistics. His manservant was instructed to prepare his favorite camel for immediate departure. It would be a long journey that would commence before dawn on the following morn.

Nigel was not the most attractive camel in the herd but this was a good thing. After all, they would spend many lonely nights on the trail and he wouldn't want to confuse the animal with his first wife, Francesca Camilleri, who he had purchased from an Italian merchant in Marrakech. Of course, in those days, she didn't have a camel mustache, which was now quite noticeable.

Being a Bedouin, the word 'urgency' was not to be found in his dictionary. Thus, the initial part of the journey was punctuated with pit-stops at various caravan layovers. Tribal gossip was passed around the camp fire and many gallons of yak-milk were consumed during the various talk-fests. Eventually, the camel and his companion arrived in Casablanca, a city that was not unknown to Hakim. His grandfather had been the piano tuner at Rick's Café Américain during the Second World War. There was a rumor that he had also been involved with the black (and white) market: ebony and ivory, I expect. He was certainly one of the usual suspects that the gendarmes periodically rounded up.

Al-Aleem Logistics had a branch office in Casablanca and the site manager was delighted to provide food and lodging for the boss. Hakim was patronized with gratuitous superlatives that were completely lacking in sincerity: an ass-kisser of the highest order. The man was a happy chappy but every time he smiled with that toothless mouth of his, you reached to check that your wallet was still in place. At least, Nigel was having a good time. Out back in the stable, they were preparing for a camel train the next day and Dolly, who was a single-hump dromedary, received a second one that night, courtesy of Nigel. There was still a little life in the old dog, yet.

The ferry from Morocco to Gibraltar is never going to take long but it becomes immeasurably longer if you travel Camel Class. Hakim decided to move to the lounge and play some Chemin de Fer, whatever that was. He was decidedly unlucky because this English fop called James Bond seemed to win every hand and he had a credit line that seemed to be limitless. Nigel was patiently waiting for his master's return, just down the deck from Bond's Aston Martin. I don't know what he thought when he saw Hakim pour a martini glass full of Sahara sand into the luxury car's fuel tank.

The travelers didn't stay long in British or Spanish territory. They headed north-west and crossed the Portuguese border before nightfall. The fishing village of Albufeira would be their first stopover in Europe and the camel found some shade in front of an impressive building. There was a sign over the door that read *Bar*, whatever that meant. Inside, Hakim was able to quench his thirst and socialize with the locals. The publican sounded just like his young nephew, who was brought up in Liverpool.

"A pint of best bitter," he said "and you'll never walk alone." Hakim Halim didn't want to be alone.

Outside, Nigel was the center of attraction. Both locals and tourists had gathered around the animal and were poking him in the ribs and making derogatory remarks concerning his state of hygiene. There was only one thing to do and, I can tell you, that when Nigel breaks wind, crowd reduction is a given. They left him to his own devices and he was happy to be given free rein. The immediate object of his desire was a long planter box that covered the back wall of the verandah. The publican's wife had put together the most wonderful collection of pansies, petunias and other colorful flowers that you would ever hope to see. The ugly creature consumed them all in ten seconds flat. His burp of satisfaction was hardly discernable as the banging of the front door heralded Hakim's return. Thirty minutes later, a hysterical female scream vented into the night air but the man and his conveyance were long gone.

There were some thirty odd beaches in this part of the Algarve and the Arab was very impressed with the clean white sand that seemed to be a magnet for hundreds of semi-naked women. He made a mental note to discuss this phenomenon with his imam on his return but not before he could revisit the seaside to check his facts.

Nigel was more impressed with the verdant grazing pasture that they had discovered on the fairways of the region's exclusive golf courses. The duo had made a habit of setting up camp on the manicured greens and silently thanked Allah for the facilities that had obviously been flagged for their convenience. Still, Hakim was convinced that the infidels had got it wrong.

"Who needs eighteen greens? Why couldn't they halve the number of comfort stops and double the size of the ablution hole?" But he was just an ignorant Bedouin. What would he know?

Lisbon was a real eye-opener. The first major city that Hakim Halim had ever visited! The cacophony of sound was incredible and the traffic and pedestrian mass was something that he had never seen before. He understood why Dorothy had been so excited at the end of the Yellow Brick Road. The eager fellow scampered off on a tour of inspection with eyes agog. Nigel was not so enthused. He had been tethered to a parking meter on the main drag, Rua Augusto, and the parking inspectors had slapped a number of infringement notices on his rump. If he had seen them coming, he would have let fly with one of his now famous wet farts but you don't see them, do you? They are worse than the Gestapo.

Hakim returned five hours later with three buddies in tow. They were all drunk and singing football songs that appeared to be offensive. Evidently, his master had offered his new-found friends a ride home but Nigel was having none of it. Every time one of them attempted to mount, the wily animal shifted his position and they sprawled onto the pavement. Even the parking inspectors, who saw an opportunity to move the beast on, tried to help but to no avail.

Eventually, the amigos went their own way and so did Hakim and Nigel. In Estoril, the pair stopped to wonder at yet another impressive building that loomed large in front of them: surely, the local mosque. In point of fact, it was the casino.

"It is time to rest our weary bodies, my noble animal friend. Why don't you find a nice grassy patch and I will pay my respects to the landlord of this fine palace."

In the absence of James Bond and other legendary card sharks, Hakim got lucky and in no time at all, had accumulated great riches and a lot of new friends who knew how to spend other people's money. Naturally, Allah would want him to share his good fortune and so the benevolent Bedouin lived high on the hog for a few days before realizing that he was on a pilgrimage and that these types of diversions were unacceptable. He was also pretty sure that his imam would not approve.

Having taken you so far with this inspirational tale of one man's awakening, I feel rather embarrassed that I have yet to divulge the real reason for this nomadic trip: the pilgrimage to Britain. Shamelessly, I have to tell you that it was all about football.

Having sent some of his hard-earned shekels, together with his thumbprint, to Manchester United, he immediately became an international member of the most powerful football team in the world. When the news broke that Wayne Rooney, their best player, was looking to move camp, Hakim was devastated and responded to the call for all supporters to come to Manchester and sign the petition for his retention.

Unbeknown to Hakim, two days after his departure, Rooney recanted and signed on for another five years. However, the Arab was already gone and you can't put the toothpaste back in the tube (apologies to Colgate Palmolive).

As the travelers headed into Spain and moved north, there was little news of the Premier League as the locals were still high from their World Cup victory. Only Spanish super stars (Rafael Nadal/Fernando Alonso/Sergio Garcia) populated the sport pages of the daily newspapers. There was another sporting attraction peculiar to people in this area and the North Africans were about to find out about it in the most unfortunate circumstances.

Nigel's radar must have been a little off because he couldn't find one of those nice green golf courses for their usual stopover. However, there was this empty oval area in the middle of nowhere. It was almost surrounded by some kind of seating arrangement that no-one had taken advantage of. The whole place was eerily silent and therefore an ideal spot for some chow and a bit of a kip. Hakim lit a fire and shared his chorizo sausage with the camel. He was extremely tired and it wasn't long before the intrepid traveler was in a deep sleep.

Now, I don't know about you but I am one that is opposed to early morning starts to sporting events. However, in Spain, they like to get things over with before it gets too hot. You also have to remember that they all have a siesta in the afternoon.

Hakim awoke to an ear-piercing, synchronized chant that was totally foreign to him – *Olé!* He rubbed his eyes in disbelief but this was no mirage. Those hitherto empty seats were now overflowing with humanity and the occupants were raucous, gleeful and manic, if not downright bloodthirsty. *Olé, olé, olé* they screamed with monotonous regularity. The hot breath that suddenly lashed the back of his exposed neck sent a chill down Hakim Halim's spine. From the corner of his eye, he saw the camel depart the scene in haste. Man's best friend was looking after number one.

It was a pity that Hakim couldn't read Spanish because there were signs all around the arena that proclaimed that this was Plaza de Toros, the bullring. I don't claim to be able to understand Arabic but when he turned around to face the beast, I believe that his words were "Oh no! This is bullshit." In fact, the shit was his and there was jelly where his legs used to be.

It's hard to know what to do when you are rooted in fear and your legs will not move; not that running would have been a good move, anyway. They were eyeballing each other and the bull was pawing the ground. Some sort of conciliation might be appropriate if it were possible. Perhaps Hakim thought that he had a way with animals.

It is always easy to be judgmental but, quite frankly, I would never have waved that red Keffiyah headdress at the animal. The brute charged and Hakim found himself in mid-air and half way to the Promised Land. Fortunately, the matadors intervened and distracted the bull while the medics dragged the hapless squatter from his camping ground.

Mercifully, the physical damage was restricted to lacerations but Hakim spent the next ten days in the psychiatric ward of the local hospital. The camel was left to his own devices and roamed aimlessly around the municipality, picking up a further fifteen parking infringements. When it was time to move on, they headed north through some of Spain's most revered destinations: the university town of Salamanca, Camino de Santiago, the Way of Saint James and Burgos, the resting place of the heroic El Cid. They picked their way through the Cantabrian Mountains, both somber and silent and obviously mentally damaged by the alarming experience that they had left behind. They even passed through Bilbao without visiting the Guggenheim. Can you believe that?

"Hey, Nigel! Look, the Guggenheim." Nigel trudged on, relentlessly: devoid of all enthusiasm and artistic commitment.

It wasn't long before they were in Basque country and San Sebastian loomed large on the horizon: a welcome stopover, to be sure. Along the way, Hakim had met Teresa, Maria, Juanita and Conchita. He was hanging out for just one margarita, chilled or frozen.

Some of you may be impressed that this durable duo had more or less taken a direct route from Casablanca to Manchester and although there had been detours to visit casinos, beaches and bars, Nigel's radar has been pretty well spot on. Given that there has been no reference to maps or compass, you've got to think that the camel is some smart animal. In fact, I'm thinking that you might think that he is smarter than his master.

What you have to understand is that there is a bond between a Bedouin and his camel. It is a bond that is based on trust and understanding. Somehow, their lines of communication are never sullied by confusion and thus, they rarely get lost. Nine times out of ten, Nigel will make the right decision. Unfortunately, there comes a time when that one out of ten comes along.

Hakim and Nigel

Hakim had been looking forward to their arrival in San Sebastian as the place boasted three glorious beaches, an aquarium and a much talked about naval museum. Admittedly, he didn't know what a naval museum was and thought that it might have something to do with those semi-naked girls that seemed to frequent the golden sands of this astonishing country. As enthusiastic as he was, he could not stay awake for the grand entrance to the Basque capital. He was napping when the camel arrived at the fork in the road.

I don't know why Nigel decided to take the path to Pamplona. He was obviously unfamiliar with this city, its rich history and the annual tradition that is embraced by lunatic adventurers, worldwide: the running of the bulls. The lines are a little blurred as to whether this festive occasion is actually a religious event or just a tourism magnet. Nevertheless, when the travelers arrived at the outskirts of the city, celebrations were in full swing and the Bedouin was not out of place with his red Keffiyah. All participants in the Bull Run are required to wear scarves of the same blood color.

It was actually the stench from the animals that stirred the man from his slumber atop the camel. Noses tend to recognize a repetitive aroma and just as we all know bullshit when we hear it, the same can be said about the smell. In the blink of an eye, Hakim was gripped with fear and trepidation and for good reason. Nigel had just turned into Santo Domingo, which is in the old part of the city, when they witnessed the most fearsome sight they had ever seen. Coming towards them at an alarming rate were thousands of screaming runners, with the herd in hot pursuit. To add to the confusion, there were urgers with sticks, oxen with bells and frenetic onlookers, who provided encouragement from behind the safety of steel barriers.

For the Arab and his friend, there was no way out. They were trampled on without fear or favor but can be grateful that the bulls passed them by without recognizing a former adversary. However, medical assistance was needed and, once again, Hakim found himself in a Spanish hospital, a little bit more banged up than last time. There were multiple contusions and he also had a broken leg. Rehabilitation would take some time and so he was resigned to a lengthy stay in the hospice but it was not all bad news.

His Arab friend from New York heard about his dilemma and paid for a short-term subscription to the local cable network. Hakim was able to keep up with all the sporting news. He discovered that Wayne Rooney was back in the fold and in fact was in scintillating form. The pilgrimage was no longer necessary. The Boston Red Sox were not doing so well so he decided to divert his interest to basketball and the Chicago Bulls. How ironic!

After a while, the authorities arranged to transport Hakim back home and he was able to limp back to the Sahara and his fourteen wives. Unfortunately, he was unable to regroup with Nigel and this was a gut-wrenching parting of the ways. The Ayuntamiento had sold the animal on the open market in order to recoup outstanding parking fines and the camel was purchased by an advertising executive from an American tobacco company, who re-named him Chuck. He was later on-sold to a rather edgy TV station for a kiddy's television show.

"Hello children. This is Billy Bo Bo and his best friend Chuck, the camel. Today, we're going to visit a brothel. Do you know what a brothel is?"

Believe it or not, this program lasted longer than it should have and they gave the camel tenure of a small allotment at the back of the studio. Every year, the station receives a small box of Sahara sand from the Al-Aleem Logistics Company, to be delivered to Chuck's alter ego, Nigel. Hakim Halim often includes a photo of Dolly, the dromedary and her most attractive calf, Nigella.

Well, what do you expect if you get mixed up with an advertising camel?

BRONNIE

The church was full to overflowing. The death of a national icon! As the service concluded, the mourners spewed onto the forecourt and pavement in the traditional manner of those who have paid their respects and must move on. With the big doors opened wide, the final hymn, *Jerusalem*, escapes its gloomy confines and pervades the pedestrian traffic of inner London.

So begins and ends David Puttnam's classic film *Chariots of Fire*. Few would begrudge it the accolades that the production received. The film was nominated for seven academy awards and won four. British Olympians still take inspiration from the deeds of Harold Abrahams and Eric Liddell, the Scottish preacher who ran like hell for the glory of God.

Abrahams was a Cambridge man but unlike some of those who followed him (Kim Philby, James Bond) he didn't go into the spying business. At least, I don't think so. It is true that he used to sing a bit and was keen on Gilbert and Sullivan but that was acceptable for a Jew in England during the early twenties. It is well documented that Harold had to fight anti-Semitism and the bureaucracy on his way to competing in the Olympic Games. After beating them all and the other competitors, he decided to become a Roman Catholic. Go figure.

My own personal favorite was Lord Lindsey, the hurdler. The man had a lot of class and a lot of money. I nearly threw up when I saw him in training with glasses of Champagne on each hurdle. What if he had knocked one over? The producers have obviously taken a few liberties with some of their facts in this film but why not? I know that our close buddy Derek Da Silva, who was the under-five sprinting champion at his kindergarten, would have doubled his efforts had there been a gallon of ice-cold creamy soda at the finish line.

For an athlete, Derek didn't have a very athletic body. His feet were too big and his arms were too small. Quite frankly, he was a runt. He was also totally inexperienced in every aspect of life. When the time came for DDS to celebrate his forthcoming nuptials, he was the only virgin at the bachelor party. The lad was definitely betrothed before his time but I think that he had correctly assessed that he may never get another chance. The bird in hand was a sweet little thing called Bronwyn, who mainly existed on a vegetarian diet of mung beans and soy milk products. She didn't drink or smoke and was almost as sexually ignorant as he was. I would have loved to be a fly on the wall during their wedding night.

"Please be gentle, my love."

"Don't worry, darling. They don't call me *Delicate Derek* for nothing."

You may wonder why I have dismissed Derek's formative years as not being worthy of comment. The fact is that they weren't. His academic record was poor and although he maintained his devotion to track and field, his exploits were good rather than outstanding. It was only after sweet Bronwyn took control of his life that he tried to make something of himself. His bride would say to him:

"Do you want to be the puffy-faced Paki from the deli or the dasher from Dagenham?"

Harold Abrahams did not become a national icon on the back of his track deeds alone. He became a mentor to Roger Bannister, who was the first person to break the four-minute mile and was regarded as the voice of athletics over many years. Bronwyn didn't aspire to those lofty heights but she did see a lot of potential in her man and, being a typical woman, set out to improve his track record. You know how it is. You never do anything right until you meet the little gal who can make it all possible.

When Derek stopped making his regular appearance at the pub, we realized that his circle of friends had been upgraded (we hoped, against his will). As it turned out, he was now completely teetotal and, as for those Friday night curries, just forget it. The Da Silva family was now buying mung beans in bulk and Bronwyn had drawn up a diet regime for him that would terrify most clear-thinking individuals. Over at the Ilford Institute if Indolence, the lad's lazy coach saw Bronnie arriving in her leg warmers and promptly resigned. Mrs Da Silva challenged her husband to prove himself. If he couldn't beat her over the sprint distance, she would be the one to appoint a new coach for the puffy-faced Paki from Dagenham.

Bronwyn not only toweled Derek over the dash but ran away from him over the hurdle course. He was flabbergasted. She duly appointed herself as his new coach. The lady was no shrinking violet and was brutally frank with the vanquished.

"You can't hack it over the shorts, honey bun. Why don't we concentrate on the distance events?"

That's exactly what they did. It would mean that she had to put a lot more miles into those skinny legs of his but little Miss Know-it-all was already mapping out a daily torture test. He managed to just get by although he nearly passed out from exhaustion, any number of times. Derek kept himself going by dreaming of seven large lagers in a row, all paid for by his friends. What a dreamer!

Herb Elliot, the Australian miler, used to train on the sand dunes at one of Melbourne's coastal resorts. At the time, this was regarded as quite eccentric. Bronnie decided to try something similar. In-between his deli duties, Derek worked as a sanitation officer for the Borough of Barking and Dagenham. The lady had him scaling the council rubbish dump on a daily basis. Wearing only his Wellington boots and work shorts, he would scamper over the refuse like a cat on a hot tin roof. The stronger the smell, the faster he ran in order to leave it all behind. If his coach thought that he was slacking, she would delay his departure until after the garbage had been delivered from the fish market. Needless to say, his workmates all thought that he was barking mad.

The first real test of his ability would come with the Grand Prix meeting at Crystal Palace. This is an annual event that can take you from a wannabe to a could-be. In the past, the track stars from Ilford had never performed well, thus the disparaging moniker *The Ilford Indolents*. It surprised no-one that Derek was unable to improve their record and finished last. He claimed that he didn't feel at home in the absence of garbage. However, the sucker for punishment had also entered for a longer event and Bronnie was going to pace him over a fast mile before the next day's events had begun. Unaware that she was being watched from the grandstand, Bronwyn left him on the turn and powered away to win by many lengths. This was pretty much the end of his career and the start of hers.

"That little girl over there has got some form."

"What, she's been to prison?"

"No, you idiot. She just broke the track record."

For almost six years, the most dominant female British athlete had been Morgana Morgan, an enigmatic distance runner from Wales. She was competitive over eight hundred meters, unbeatable over the metric mile and totally impressive when she elected to compete in the five thousand meter event. One of those interested spectators in the grandstand was her ex-coach, the brilliant but erratic Klaus Wunderlich. He had split with the talented miler because of creative difference with her life partner, the very difficult to understand Gruffudd Llewellyn-Jones.

What Wunderlich saw of Bronnie impressed him. She was a small package but her legs were lithe and muscular, there was no excess poundage on her ass and her gently heaving breasts made his heart beat faster. He wondered who the puffy-faced Paki was.

A few hours later, Klaus approached Bronwyn in the cafeteria and told her that he liked her form. Derek subsequently hit him with his famous Rawalpindi Right Cross, a boxing move that had been taught to him by his relatives from the old country. Although Klaus boasted a lineage that went all the way back to the Hitler youth, he accepted his chastisement in good faith and patiently explained his credentials to the young couple.

He wanted to take on the young runner and, although the Olympic Games were fast approaching, he maintained that he could get her up for the trials, which were more imminent. He mentioned nothing about his strident desire to be instrumental in unseating his former charge from her throne as the Empire's favorite female athlete.

The lady in question was already in training and had set up camp in her home town of Llanfairpwllgwyngyllgogerychwyrndrobwllllantysil-iogogogoch. You may not be able to get a handle on the pronunciation of this little village but most know it as the town with the longest name in Britain. In fact, Morgana first came to prominence as a schoolgirl, when she became the first person to run the length of the town signpost without oxygen.

Klaus was a hard task-master and sacrifices would have to be made by both Bronwyn and Derek. However, Derek was not happy when the high profile coach moved in with them and proceeded to turn their life upside-down. First to go were the mung beans, which turned out to be not as nutritious as first thought. Sauerkraut and German sausage became the stable diet. This fare wasn't nutritious either but Klaus liked them so that was that. Bronnie embraced all the coach's demands and it wasn't long before she was showing tremendous improvement on the track. In fact, she beat just about everybody who mattered but, wisely, Klaus kept her away from Morgana. The showdown would not happen until the Olympic trials. What a showdown it was.

"Now Bronnie, don't be nervous. Just run to the best of your ability. All we have to do is qualify." Klaus said that as if it were a foregone conclusion. Bronnie would definitely be nervous.

The day of the fifteen hundred meter final was warm and sunny and a great crowd turned out. There had been a bit of a buzz about the newcomer from Dagenham but all eyes were on the lass from Llanfairpwllgwyngllgogerychwyrndrobwllllantysiliogogogoch. A female choir sang *Women of Harlech* and they were joined by Tom Jones and Catherine Zeta-Jones for a reprise. Morgana received messages of good luck from Anthony Hopkins, Shirley Bassey, Bonnie Tyler and Charlotte Church.

The odds were stacked against Bronwyn Da Silva from the start. Nevertheless, the Institute of Indolence was represented and Derek brought along the whole darts team from his local. Since his retirement, he had reverted back to his old ways and life was good again.

The honey blonde from the Glasgow Temperance Society led them out and maintained her lead for two laps. At this stage, Morgana cruised up to them and increased the pace. Only Bronwyn was able to sustain her momentum and moved in behind the leader. It became a two-girl race but, alas, the hopes of all Barking and Dagenham supporters were dashed as the Welsh rabbit skipped away to win by half the straight. Both girls were under the Olympic qualifying time so it was drinks all around. The Scottish lass failed to finish and was last seen crying into her milk.

Klaus could see that there was work to be done but there was still time as the Games were some time off. Unfortunately, Bronnie would now operate under the auspices of an official team coach and he would work in the background. This was the situation that also applied to Harold

Abrahams, during the lead-up to the Paris Olympics. His coach was a professional and was banned from attending the amateur Games.

Around this time, on the other side of the world, qualifying events were also taking place in Brisbane, Australia. At the Wooloongabba Oval, a laconic aboriginal girl from Dumbleyung had smashed the Commonwealth record and made it look easy. She ran barefoot and there was a stampede by prospective sponsors to sign her up. The media had baptized her *The Dumbleyung Dazzler*.

Back home in Old Blighty, the Olympic team had been invited to Buckingham Palace and Bronnie was delighted that she was able to press the flesh with the monarch. There were many famous people at the garden party and she even met the fabled entrepreneur Richard Branson, who was flying friends and relatives to the Games for free, if they were eligible to utilize his new travel company, Virgin Airlines. Derek's two brothers were overjoyed.

There were still a number of meetings that were to be held in Europe before the athletes were due on the big stage and each time Bronnie managed to bridge the gap, little by little. She was now a serious chance of a gold medal. Her state of mind was also in good shape which was not the case with her immediate opponent. Morgana Morgan's life partner, Gruffudd Llewellyn-Jones, had been found *in flagrante* with a Bavarian beer hall beauty. He claimed that he had been seduced against his will and that the drugs weren't his. In the lady's lederhosen, they found a check signed by Klaus Wunderlich. Dirty deeds over the distance!

Finally, the big day arrived and it would be nothing like any of them had seen before. One hundred thousand people were packed liked sardines into the arena and the limits of the stadium capacity were stretched. Not that they were there to see the final of the women's distance event. It was the last day of competition and a dozen Playboy Bunnies were going to parachute into the arena with fire extinguishers. It was hoped that one of them would be able to douse the Olympic flame and conclude the athletic hostilities.

By the way, Bronwyn Da Silva managed the silver. The gold medal was won by the Aussie girl and poor Morgana was beaten into third place by a German runner from Bavaria.

This wasn't the end of Bronnie's career. In fact, she represented Great Britain in two more Olympic renewals: the last as a five thousand meter competitor. She was able to add another silver medal to her collection and retired as one of the most loved and revered athletes in the country. She wasn't so loved at home. Eventually, Derek tired of it all and ran off with a female member of his darts team. The divorce was quick and final and Bronnie decided to marry Klaus. He was considerably older but she had become addicted to sauerkraut and loved his German sausage. They had two kids: Adolf and Herman.

Don't you just love a story with a happy ending?

The silver medalist!

TYRONE

Have you ever had trouble getting into your jeans? You should try getting into someone else's jeans. Rosie Clutterbuck was quite adamant that you are supposed to get permission to do something like that. After a few more of these kinds of episodes, I ended up in a reform school. It wasn't so bad. Really! The other kids were great fun, the dormitory was clean and the chef was a better cook than my mom.

Now, I know that you are going to think that this is another sad tale about me and my misguided youth. Not so. I don't like to talk about my early days in America. This is an almost unbelievable tale about one of my room-mates, Tyrone Timberwater, who lobbed at the borstal institution a few months before my arrival. Ty was raised in the lower east side of Manhattan by a family that definitely had confused genes. Although it was not exactly a ghetto, it was a tough working class neighborhood. His first given name, Vincent, had been a tribute to the saintly protector of the poor and downtrodden but his star-struck mother was smitten by the latest Hollywood heart-throb, Tyrone Power and so the saintly identity was superseded.

By the time that Ty had slipped through the welcoming doors of our home away from home, he had a rap sheet that made for some very ugly reading. His most repetitive charge was for assault and battery and his weapon of choice was his Uncle Milt's baseball bat; not that Milton had ever used it. The sports freak had purchased the instrument of pain at a pawn shop, where it was purported to be a Babe Ruth cast-off from when he was a pitcher for the Boston Red Sox. This was a total red herring. He should have gone to a Jewish pawn shop: expensive but kosher.

Occasionally, we got to see Ty in action and one could only marvel at his aggressive swing and perfect timing, probably brought about by his precise hand to eye co-ordination. The matron of the infirmary was not a fan as she had to patch up the wounded. However, she did have a sense of humor and partitioned a Ty Timberwater wing for his victims.

Needless to say, the authorities did not take kindly to his bully-boy attitude and we all suffered because of it. Because of the manner in which he metered out punishment, baseball was banned as an option in our sports program and all the equipment was donated to the local Saint Vincent de Paul recycling outlet. How poignant was that?

It is hard to believe that this decision changed his life but it did. The youth was an absolute coward without the deterrent that only a big stick can provide and so he looked for a substitute weapon of destruction. When the warden's favorite seven iron went missing from his golf bag, no-one thought to look under Ty's mattress. The warden was only a small person but he did have a fiery temper.

"If the juvenile delinquent who stole my property doesn't return it within twenty-four hours, there will be no privileges for a month."

Of course, most of the lads had no idea what had been stolen, so the next morning, when he arrived at his office, he found seventy-five previously stolen items outside his door. The golf club was not amongst them.

Until his eventual release, Ty remained the go-to man in terms of dispute arbitration and his trusty short iron was never far from his side. The staff at the facility was never able to pin the theft on him and it gave him immense satisfaction to learn that the warden's game completely imploded, as his replacement club proved to be hopeless in his hands.

When the time came for Tyrone's redeployment into society, the warden had been impressed by his new-found knowledge of the golf game and pulled some strings to get him a job at a Long Island private club. He would be the new junior assistant professional and would get weekly tuition from the legendry pro, a kindly soul who enthusiastically supported the redemption of wayward youth. However, to be on the safe side, the cash takings were always under the control of the senior assistant pro.

You may think that a posh country club on Long Island would make Ty feel like a duck out of water but this was not so. Back in the 'hood, one came across liars, cheats, fraudsters and stand-over men on a daily basis. These people had now progressed through many levels of prosperity and quite a few had decided to reward their legitimacy by taking up golf. Actually, he felt quite at home.

As junior assistant pro, the lad had to accept all the menial tasks. These little jobs were hand-passed to him with great regularity by his immediate superior, who was both lazy and talentless. Ty walloped him consistently, whether the game was Stroke, Stableford, Scramble, Best Ball or Bingo Bango Bongo (don't ask).

There were a number of elderly matrons in the club who were still trying to come to terms with the game but they were nothing if not enthusiastic. Ty soon became their mentor and they all fussed over him. We are talking about people with names like Rockefeller, Vanderbilt, Rothschild and Kennedy. Mrs Kennedy, a distant relative of you know who, invited him to a Boston tea party and a Cape Cod fishing trip. How good was that?

"Hey, kid. You are using that reel like a *Red Sox* slugger. Here, let me show you."

"Thanks, Senator. Finesse was never my strong point."

Tyrone was quite a personable chap and he eventually won the admiration and respect of all members. He was club champion for three years in a row and they still talk about some of his wonderful seven iron shots. It was his rescue club. He always turned to it whenever he was in trouble. Eventually, Ty couldn't resist the urge to join the professional tour and he left Long Island with fond memories, a fat address book and a bulging wallet. There was no underestimating the challenge ahead and he would need every bit of that nest egg to survive in such a spirited environment.

I suppose I should explain that you don't just walk into the professional golf circuit in America. The starting point is a very competitive index rating and then you have to impress in various qualifying tournaments. That he breezed through and over these hurdles was testament to his ability. It wasn't long before Ty was winning over the fans with his stylish stroke play and rakish charm. Of course, this kind of adulation can be a poisoned chalice for one so young.

I can relate to this fact. I used to be the undisputed ping pong champion over at the 47th Street Youth Center and all the girls were there for the taking. Well, all except Rosie Clutterbuck, who, as it turned out, was a probationary nun from the local convent. Nevertheless, she had a great backhand and I believe that she used it effectively in her long and distinguished teaching career.

"Quite frankly, Mother Superior, it was only a small slap and I didn't expect him to arrive at school with his lawyer, the next day. Really, I don't know what this world is coming to."

It is true to say that Ty didn't have the same charisma with women that I did but he was still a bit of a mover and there were any number of groupies that followed the tour. They are a totally different demographic to those who you would find at a Pearl Jam concert and, in fact, some of them have probably passed their use-by date. Ty's caddy calls them the cow pats: the older they are, the easier to pick up.

Ruby Rose Ratskeller was a scribe with one of the New York dailies and her brief was simple. Get the stories that will make the readers sit up and take notice and do whatever it takes. Ruby took these instructions literally and her briefs were found in other people's hotel rooms from Seattle to San Jose. She was five feet seven and her legs went all the way to heaven. Ty would be a pushover. He had just scored his first hole-in-one at the illustrious seventh hole at Pebble Beach and his magnificent tee-shot had cost the tournament sponsor a brand new sports car. All he needed was a good sport to help him road test it.

I can only imagine what went on that day and night between the two of them. The next day he forfeited his lead and, in fact, failed to make the cut. People have remarked that it was strange that he still had a grin on his face as he was usually a bit grumpy when he lost. It was a few weeks later that he found himself on the cover of the Sunday Magazine, described as the sportsman most likely. It was all there: the deprived upbringing, the institutional sentence and the reformation. He was sure that his conversations with Ruby Rose had been off-the-record. Then again, perhaps he was talking in his sleep. All the same, he wasn't displeased. The national publicity had given him a degree of notoriety and his fan base swelled considerably. A further two sponsors came on board to confirm his consumer appeal. Ty was now earning big bucks.

When you are making big money in this business, your personal staff numbers increase and so do you professional affiliations. Ty's spin doctors pounced on the circumstances of his tragic life story and converted it into a redemption tale of almost unbelievable proportions. In fact, there were many who doubted most of it. They pointed to his time at Long Island and surmised that he was just another rich kid who was pampered into prosperity. Then the truth came out. The newspaper was inundated with letters and emails from those who had been brutalized by Tyrone Timberwater. He was called a ruffian and a hooligan and one such correspondent included a photo of his scarred head featuring an indelible number seven. The warden would now know what had happened to his lost golf club.

This kind of revelation can sometimes douse one's popularity but in Ty's case it only magnified the mystique. There was a new catch-cry to be found on the links. Instead of *in the hole* the spectators were now shouting *use your seven iron*. As often as not he obliged and the legend lived on. He was pulling the crowds big time and his sponsors were very grateful. Versace designed a *Brutality* line of sports clothes for the fans and American Express presented him with a new seven iron. It was twenty-four carat gold and so valuable that he was afraid to leave home without it.

Doris Nightingale had been a waitress in the spike bar for about three months when she first met Ty. Obviously, I cannot divulge which particular club I am talking about but the prices were not cheap. Certainly not as cheap as Dippy Doris! She was a bright, chatty little thing and I don't know why they called her that but they did. Actually, she was not such a little thing and I don't think that she had breast implants. I do know that she could never completely button her blouse and this was most disconcerting when she was leaning over the table with the sandwiches. Who knows when Ty decided that it would be a good idea to doodle Doris but sure enough, he got her in the Ti-tree behind the seventeenth green on a balmy summer night in mid-July. It became a ritual that was repeated whenever the lad was in town between tournaments.

The thing about having it off with the staff is that you'll never be able to keep a lid on it. Having access to gossip is essential in the hospitality industry and there would be few who couldn't give birth to a rumor within minutes of conception. With the advent of *Facebook* and *Twitter*, all the sordid details can be confirmed to five hundred countries before you've pulled your pants up. Of course, Ty regretted his actions but he took so long to contemplate his regrets, time overtook him. Doris confided that she was pregnant and, to this day, she can count herself lucky. His faithful seven iron was nowhere in sight.

Today, Dippy Doris has her own bar in Sao Paulo, Brazil, where young Niblick runs amok amongst the customers. He is an absolute delight and all the patrons love to interact with the little fellow. The business is not a great money-spinner but all her bills are picked up by an off-shore company and Versace underwrites her clothing allowance. Ty always calls the tyke at Christmas and even sent him some autographed golf balls for his third birthday, whoever John Smith is.

In South America, they have had a few golf champions but their main go is football. Very much like my own country, where the tabloids absolutely live off the sport. *Joe Bloggs Wins MVP Award* the headline will scream. You have to turn the page to find any worthwhile news like *Destruction of Earth Imminent*. I guess you have to look after the fans and the sponsors but I think that Ty's sponsors were looking after themselves. However, I think that they copped more than they bargained for. Over the next few years, there was a child in Bangkok and another in Botswana, who really stood out in his Versace gold lamé nappies. Ty just couldn't keep it in his pants and the family of man was expanding at a great rate.

On the golf course, records were broken and a living legend was created. He was creaming them on six continents and his appearance fees were now higher than the gross national product of the average African oligarchy. By the time Ty was thirty-five years of age, there was hardly anything that he hadn't done, although the new country club in Antarctica was a bit of a challenge. He designed the layout but because of local rules, it wasn't a sanctioned PGA course.

"Hey Ty, there's a whale in the middle of the fairway."

'That's OK. You can take a drop."

Club Antarctica

It's hard to know where he goes from here. When you've got it all, what can go wrong? His victims from days gone by have long forgiven him. Even my friend, Sister Rosie Clutterbuck, has his picture in her breviary and I thought that I was her favorite male. I certainly hope that there was no assignation there. There is a definite limit to God's capacity for forgiveness.

Heaven's above! The odds of Ty getting through the Pearly Gates would be very long. I once discussed the matter with him and he maintained that both he and Saint Peter came from the same borough in New York and that would count for a lot. He was unaware that there were other churches and basilicas that were named after the good shepherd in other parts of the world. All the same, it is often said that even God can't hit a one iron and Ty's teaching experience would be invaluable.

Let's not get ahead of ourselves. The man has many good years ahead of him and I hope that I can remain on the payroll as his confidante, spin doctor, gambling advisor and diarist. After all, the story always needs to be told and what would you think of him, without my compassionate explanations? As I have often said, the road is hard and long and one always needs to keep their eye upon the donut and not the hole; unless you are a golfer or a sewerage contractor. Either way, you are involved in a crapshoot and the best man doesn't always win.

I can remember when our boy was three strokes behind with two holes to play in the Players' Championship. His opponent reached into his bag and came out with a cobra. The snake scuttled away without biting him but he had a heart attack and expired on the spot. This meant back-to-back tournament wins for Ty. Seven days earlier, he had won the New Delhi Open in India.

All this world travel might make some of you a bit envious but it is hard work. The flying is tedious, the change in weather conditions can sometimes be debilitating and often the good-time girls don't speak a word of English. Yes, of course there are good-time girls. Ty needs to be completely relaxed before competition and I need something to do while he is playing golf. However, this is something that I am going to keep to myself. You can imagine what would happen if details of these kinds of escapades ever got out.

People have often suggested that I write a book about some of the people that I know. Tyrone Timberwater would certainly qualify as one of my most interesting friends. Whether or not it is a sympathetic narrative is immaterial. Through adversity, one can rise to great heights if you have the steely determination to succeed and total confidence in yourself and your abilities.

Ty is still winning tournaments and his twenty-four carat gold seven iron is as accurate as ever. He passed on the original Borstal club to his Uncle Milt, who proudly mounted it above his fireplace. It is only a matter of time before he flogs it to his favorite pawn shop.

PEST AGAIN: A SOBER REFLECTION

By now, you will be aware of the reasons for Paddy's unfortunate public image. I have done my best to steer him away from hostelries and houses of ill repute but his lapses of judgment are only accentuated by my own failure to keep him on a righteous path. After all, if you want to be a role-model, you can't be a drunk and a rake can you?

I have searched through my chronicles and sought to discover some stories that might put Mr Pest in a good light. If you ignore his unfortunate gambling habits, I think that I have found some. Paddy is the perennial traveler and he has a lot to offer those who are contemplating a trip for the first time. In fact, once he has got this crime thing out his system, he could well become a travel guide.

I expect his most potent advice would be:

"Avoid the pubs with no cheer."

THE GREASY POLE

I have told this story before as an illustration of the inquisitive nature of most Australians. It was our turn to host the Olympic Games and, in all modesty, we did ourselves proud. I accosted this athletic looking fellow outside one of the stadiums.

"Are you a pole-vaulter?" I asked.

"Yes," he replied. "But how did you know my name was Walter?"

Until I arrived in Cracow, he was one of the few Polish people that I have had much to do with. Of course, there was George the Pole, Andrew the Pole and Olga, the pole dancer. Not that I knew that particular lady all that well. I was ejected from Olga's work place because I nicked twenty dollars from her knickers but I don't know what all the fuss was about. I was going to re-circulate it through the establishment's refreshment outlet, anyway.

Cracow is a university city and, as such, one tends to slink around the various campus sites while trying to whisper at the top of your voice. Well, you know what I mean. There is a bit of reverence about the place. The young men are very vibrant and energetic and the women are almost universally attractive. Perhaps that is why I didn't want to leave.

During our farewell drinks session in Sydney, Olga had given me her little sister's address. I was gobsmacked to discover that she was an A-grade student with an alert mind and a passion for knowledge. I also noted with obvious satisfaction that she had nice tits, tight buns and a killer smile. Sabina and her sister were Poles apart so I decided to be on my best behavior. I played up the fact that one of my relatives once met Karol Wojtyła, the former Archbishop of Cracow and late of the Vatican. This impressed her and I am glad that I mentioned it before I told her that her sister was a pole dancer.

"I'm sorry to tell you this, Sabina, but your sister is not in a good place. However, she makes lots of money and doesn't need a clothing allowance."

Olga without her pole

In America, *get out of here* is an exclamation remark of surprise. In Poland, when used with anger and venom, it means get out of here. I got out of there, fast. For some reason, she blamed me for the degradation and immoral decline of her sibling. Given that we had just met, I was totally impressed by the accuracy of her character assessment. I moved on.

I was hoping to tell you so much more about this wonderful city but I never know how to navigate past their impossible names. Needless to say, the architecture is superb and the city area is jammed with Renaissance, Baroque and Gothic structures that almost defy description. Anyway, that's my excuse. The inhabitants are mostly Catholic so there are plenty of churches for the devout tourist and lots of gardens and parks for the environmentally aware. You'll come across the dark side on your way out. Auschwitz and the salt mines provide a grim reminder of some pretty dark days in Polish history.

What can you say about history? Another time! Another place! Let's face it. If we knew then what we now know about salt, these places would never have existed. They would have been tofu mines. Apart from the first non-Italian pope in over four hundred years, the city has had some revered residents and I refer to film directors Andrzej Wajda and Roman Polanski. They have both had brilliant if not turbulent careers and chose Cracow as a place where they could find appreciation for their creative individuality.

I have yet to find such a place but I do have some empathy with those who choose to hole up with a scandalous muse in some desolate seaside hideaway. I can see how this would get the juices flowing: creative and otherwise. Roman likes his ladies young but being a superstitious gambler, I shy away from black cats and thirteen year olds. Having said all this, I might mention that those seaside hideaways around the Baltic Sea aren't exactly the same as those in Kingston, Jamaica. It can be very cold in winter. People often talk about the North Pole and the South Pole but they rarely mention the frozen Poles who frequent Gdansk, the largest port city in this region. Things do get better in summer and that is when the tourists drop by to absorb the historical ambiance of the place.

The city was formally known as Danzig and has always been a popular spot. The Germans and the Poles were always at each other's throats over ownership rights and the Russians were unwelcome intruders. Thus, the emergence of Solidarity and Lech Walesa! There are quite a number of famous people that called Gdansk home but I can't pronounce their names either – except for the cutie named Aneta, who won the Miss World competition in 1989. It was a close call but she had the right qualifications to get over the line.

"My name Aneta. I Miss Poland. 'allo."

"Yes, Aneta, I miss Poland, too but tell me; are you committed to world peace and the reduction of hunger and other humanitarian causes?"

"No, Sir. I just have big tits."

War saw a lot of destruction in the major cities of Poland and their capital, Warsaw, was not spared. This meant that re-building projects were initiated by a communist regime with the design capabilities of a peanut. Residential eyesores were erected all over the city as sacred landmarks were razed to the ground. Fortunately, not all of the historical architecture has been lost. Many buildings have been restored and the structures that endure are a delight. It was easy to demolish most of the Eastern bloc culture and so we now have a city that generates old-world charm, embellished with contemporary urban design.

They (anything you want to know for a small remuneration) tell me that there are over eighty parks and gardens in the city and I can believe that. I didn't ask why the place was called Warsaw but they told me anyway. Evidently a fisherman called Wars fell in love with a mermaid called Sawa and that was the end of the penny section. I gave the informant a few Zloty and told him to come up with something original. Blow me down if I didn't then come across a number of mermaid statues scattered throughout the city. Legend has it that one of them is related to the *Little Mermaid* in Copenhagen. It must be tough being family and not able to visit.

"Can I inform you, Mr Pest, that we have memorials to Marie Curie and Frédéric Chopin, two of our favorite sons, although Madam Curie is of the female persuasion?"

This was all very interesting but I couldn't help but think that they had forgotten to venerate one of their most durable exports – the Polish sausage. This delicacy is extremely portable and is complimentary to so many different types of liquid refreshment. You can't claim to be an experienced traveler if you haven't lunched with the locals.

"Excuse me, waiter. There's a fly on my sausage."

"No, Sir. That's a Polish albatross. We only serve flies with the Sambuca."

"Bloody Hell!"

It is a measure of my patience that I have delved so deeply into this travelogue without mentioning Piotr Piotrowski. I honor him with this minor tribute because he is a fellow bounder and a credit to his chosen profession – schnicklebusting. Of course, he likes to classify himself as an entrepreneur.

When my train arrived at Cracow station, Piotr was there to help me with my bags. There would be no charge, even though he was a struggling student with no visible means of support. Three minutes after he had introduced himself, I conservatively estimated his net wealth to be in the higher income bracket. With his easy going charm, the personal platitudes that confidently punctuated his conversation would be an irresistible

Footnote: *Sambuca with flies* is an after-dinner treat. They float three coffee beans in the anise flavored liqueur. Alternatively called *Sambuca Con Mosca*, the three beans represent health, happiness and prosperity.

magnet for any number of well-heeled travelers that passed through this busy transportation hub. If he allocated a maximum of ten minutes to me and others, I could see that he would chalk up a daily clientele of impressive numbers. Not that there would be any charge from a struggling student with no visible means of support. However, who wouldn't feel sorry for him?

For some reason, Polonia Pete saw me as more than a ten-minute client and probably felt confident that I would react favorably to his various recommendations. He had appraised the quality of my luggage and subsequently guessed which hotel rating I would require. Smart lad! Transport was no problem because his brother was already at the taxi rank and a family discount would apply. You just can't beat getting in on the ground floor can you?

It didn't take long to get down to the nitty gritty. Yes, I was a single gentlemen and a female escort would be a distinct advantage, especially if she had geographical capabilities. Piotr said that his sister was a professional virgin but she had any number of girl-friends. A friends-of-the-family concession was definitely negotiable. I think I threw him a little when I asked if his sister was available.

When you travel, it is surprising how friendly complete strangers can be. They want to know everything about you including your bank details and key codes. Wouldn't it be a hoot if your password was as silly as theirs? Because of the dangers associated with identity fraud, I like to travel with somebody else's credit card. It was a habit I got into after an intensive pick-pocketing course that I availed myself of, many years ago. There are any numbers of cards available at railway stations and airports – other people's luggage, too. I couldn't wait to get to the hotel and see what I had acquired in Cracow.

As it turned out, Piotr's sister was a stewardess with Virgin Airlines. No wonder she was such a happy person. We had arranged to meet at a bar of her choosing but, as soon as I arrived, I realized that my clerical garb was inappropriate. Sometimes you can steal the wrong luggage. Nevertheless, I tried to make the most of a difficult situation and ordered two Tequila Slammers. Most of the punters were drinking vodka but this virgin didn't fly to Mexico so a change is as good as a holiday. I didn't tell her that I had become addicted to this little nip during some jail time south of the border.

I didn't tell her a lot of things but that's the way it is when you meet somebody who is used to socializing with refined people. I always travel economy class. This whole social scenario of Polonia Pete, his sister and brother, who was now acting as chauffeur/chaperone, was based on the premise that I was a person of substance with considerable disposable income. Nobody was better placed to dispose of my income than this lot. All it takes is experience. Incidentally, the chaperone took one look at my priest's outfit and called it an early night. One up for yours truly!

I don't think that there is any need for me to elaborate any further regarding my association with the Piotrowski family. I only chronicle this brief interlude as a warning to fellow travelers who may also be side-tracked by the comfort of strangers – in Gdansk, it was a chap called Kowalski and in Warsaw, there were the Król twins. I have to tell you that this was a real class act. Charles Dickens couldn't have come up with more inventive rogues.

Hunting for rogues is my bread and butter and Paddy Pest had bigger fish to fry than these young rascals, although I did like their style. Julius Jaroslav Jablonski was a greaseball and slimebag who had terrorized Central Europe for ten years and eluded the combined forces of the French Sûreté, the Italian Polizia, the German Bundespolizei and MI6. Even Mossad had not managed to flush him out of his hideout. These people are highly professional investigators with unlimited resources and, yet, he remained at large. Somebody came up with the idea that they should find a crime fighter who was completely unprofessional and that is how I acquired the gig. At the time, I was inactive, indolent and usually in bed.

It wasn't true that Olga knew Jablonski but everyone knows that if you want to gauge public opinion, you refer to the Poles. After consultation with the lady concerned and her sister plus Polonia Pete and his family, I deduced that Big Julie was either in Cracow, Gdansk or Warsaw. Certainly, that's where the rumors were taking me.

They were wrong.

The big brute came from a small village near the Ukraine border and he wasn't that hard to track down. All those intelligence agencies must have been asleep at the wheel. Jablonski had a weakness, Polish sausage and this particular village produced the most flavorsome sausage in the whole of Jaroslaw County. I think that it had something to do with the blood that they used. Julius was a trencherman of the highest order but he was a lousy tipper. I simply followed a path of sulky waiters across Poland until I arrived at the door of Hattie's Humongous Hash House (English translation).

The big man was a master of disguise and so was I. I had ditched my religious accoutrements and now approached the bar and grill, cunningly dressed as a peasant. "Throw that peasant out of here" boomed a deep voice from within the premises and before I could properly get my bearings, I was sailing through the air en route to a nasty confrontation with some very hard cobblestones. I did, however, manage a backward glance and a parting vision of a very large man, seated at a table with half a sausage in his mouth. He was dressed like a Roman Catholic bishop.

Can you believe that? I could have maintained my original disguise and extracted a confession from him. Unfortunately, his gigantic altar boys had caused me some grief. I have been ejected from many places but this time I landed on my head and awoke in hospital. A smiling medical person appeared before my eyes.

"Don't worry, my friend. There are no broken bones and we've booked you in for every possible test. You'll be out of here within hours."

Why should I worry? They had already swiped my credit card and it appeared that they were not at all surprised that a peasant would carry an American Express Gold Card. When Mr Klingner receives his monthly transaction account, I hope they include the medical report. It will show that there were no fractures and that his dizzy spells will disappear over time. He will be so pleased. Meanwhile, I recovered control of the plastic fantastic and headed back to the bar. I had now assumed the persona of a good-time boy out on the town. No-one would be able to see through that impersonation.

It was the rush hour and trade was booming. This was not a time or place for the clergy so I could understand that Jablonski had moved on. I decided to enjoy some me-time. There were about thirty vodka variations on the menu and they all looked lethal. I settled on a Slavonicas and beckoned the food waiter.

"Where does the goulash come from?" I asked.

"Hungary," he replied.

"Of course I'm bloody hungry" I screamed, as he scurried off.

It's always the same with these waiters who can't speak English. When the cabbage rolls arrived (which I didn't order) I accepted the dish gratefully and woofed them down before confusion could reign. It was then that I met the delectable Fifi Fandoodle.

I once knew some Fandoodles in Montmartre and I wondered if she had relatives in Paris. She said that she had relatives anywhere I wanted them to be. Some women can be so accommodating, can't they? Fifi was on the wrong side of thirty but you would never know it. Her body was taut and her confident posture gave off a regimental familiarity. I was later to learn that she had been involved with quite a few regiments.

As a compassionate soul, I always like to encourage social intercourse with the locals and this was a local girl. The woman was so poor, she couldn't afford proper underwear. Obviously, Fifi had given herself some sort of stage name and the proprietor had given her a job out of pity. I guess you would categorize it as customer relations.

We shared one of those obligatory air-kisses and that was enough to send my senses into overdrive. Amidst the pungent aroma of cheap perfume, stale garlic and over-proof vodka, my alert nose picked up on a familiar fragrance: After-Shave PI. After-Shave PI is purchased in bulk by the Catholic Church and distributed world-wide to members of the clergy. It is a passion inhibitor.

It this case, it hadn't worked because it was obvious to me that Fifi Fandoodle and Bishop Julius Jablonski had been playing hide the sausage. My guess was that she was, in fact, a gangster's moll. How exciting!

There was only one thing to do. I excused myself and rang the Minister for Religious Affairs, who immediately promised me a SWAT team within the hour. When Fifi clocked off that night, I followed her to the grounds of the cathedral and sure enough, Jablonski was there with his henchmen. The real bishop was tied to a straight-backed chair in his underwear, which, I might add, seemed a bit lacier than one would have expected.

In my youth, I would have charged in with all guns blazing and probably made a mess of things. I can still make a mess of things but these days I am more circumspect. I decided to retire to a small enclave under one of the spires and wait for the cavalry to arrive. As often happens, after a long day, my eyes started to droop. All of a sudden I awoke with a start and, instinctively, grabbed for the nearest stabilizing force. Unfortunately, it was the bell rope.

As the bells tolled throughout the countryside, the villains were alerted and would probably be able to lose themselves in the throng that was now pouring into the church for evening mass.

Perhaps I had misread the criminal mind. Although self-preservation is a strong sentiment, revenge is also high on the pecking order and the bodyguards had been dispatched to do their worst. The smaller of the two gangsters was six feet five inches tall and marginally smaller than his counterpart. He suffered with an inferiority complex because of this shortcoming. Therefore, he tried harder.

I think that it was a statue of the Virgin Mary that came hurtling towards yours truly and shattered and scattered all around me. I wondered if he had been a javelin thrower at any time in his life. No matter! My hurdle form returned as I scooted over the pews to the nearest exit at the side of the church. On my departure, I discovered that the SWAT team was establishing a perimeter around the cathedral.

They managed to apprehend Big Julie, who went down mouthing obscenities at everyone, particularly me. I released the bishop from his bonds and he rewarded me with a blessing plus a promise of more heavenly favors, if I failed to remember that he was wearing lacy underwear.

When Paddy Pest ties up a case, things happen pretty quickly and such was the situation, here. There was a bit of a conundrum regarding the fate of Fifi but she was eventually released into my custody and I immediately invited her to take part in a rehabilitation program that was about to take place in Gdansk. All I needed was confirmation from the realtor that my leased cottage by the seaside was ready for habitation. The weather forecast was ten degrees below zero but we really didn't need to go outside.

Julius Jaroslav Jablonski received a twenty-five year sentence for assorted crimes and was dispatched to a dark and dank prison with extremely high walls. He would have to be a pole-vaulter to get out of there.

Julius Jablonski: the greasy Pole

UNDER THE BRIDGES OF PARIS

The door knock is an unglamorous adjunct to police work and for that reason this task is usually assigned to employees who boast the rank of constable. As Paddy Pest usually operates on a modest retainer, outside the perimeter of officialdom, I have to do these chores myself. In this case, the street of shame was the Rue de Roulette, a dark and dingy thoroughfare of dilapidated structures that housed pimps, prostitutes, actors, down-on-their-luck gamblers and freelance journalists.

The heist had taken place on Saint Vitas Day but I didn't know what to read into that. After all, Saint Vitas was the patron saint of actors, dancers, comedians and epileptics. The thieves had hit Le Louvre and removed the Mona Lisa, in one of the most daring displays of post-modern art theft in contemporary times. As you could imagine, this was big news. Well, it should have been but the museum and the insurers went into lock-down mode and I was out-sourced. The paying patrons didn't notice a thing because the burglars had replaced the painting with a substitute: a brilliant forgery that was hardly distinguishable from the original.

So, here I was on this boulevard of broken dreams, looking for a crafty American art thief of limited intelligence. I may not have mentioned the fact that although the forgery was a brilliant reproduction, it had been signed *Mona Leeza*.

There is a café/bar on almost every corner in Paris and this street was no exception. I decided that I should wet my whistle and contemplate my next move. You can sometimes be undone by a brasserie in this town. The curbside magic is wonderful but you should never waltz into the establishment, point at the pot of ale on the next table and say "I'll have one of those." When *l'addition* arrives, you'll discover that you are about to pay twenty bucks for a glass of beer. On the other corner of the street, they're doing a happy hour and you can tell by the look on the faces of the customers that they are paying no more than five dollars for the same refreshment.

From my outdoor table, I was in a strategic location to watch the comings and goings around Rue de Roulette. I do apologies for my choice of words. A young couple was having it off in a darkened doorway, not a stone's throw away from my sentinel position. I had half a mind to warn them of the dangers of having sex standing-up. It can lead to dancing. Further down the road, a couple of gendarmes had pulled over a motor cyclist on his Harley Davidson. My score was hogs 1 pigs 2.

I was fast coming to the conclusion that I might have to actually do some door knocking when a suspicious movement caught my attention. A banging shutter alerted my senses and, then, in the twinkling of an eye, I noticed a furtive figure descend down a stoop, into the street and walk off quickly. He was carrying a cylindrical package under his arm. I could almost smell the Mona Lisa.

There is an art to tailing somebody and, in doing so, most intelligence agencies adopt various tactics. I prefer the basic model, which was first put into operation some time during the dark ages. Because there was little light, you avoided losing your target by getting as close as possible and you then hung on like a leech. I settled into a position not far behind this dude, who had no idea that he was being followed. In fact, he was no longer furtive and was whistling a Broadway melody. How easy was this going to be?

The young man's destination was a surprise. We were in the 6th *arrondissement* and outside the historical Abbey of Saint-Germain-des-Prés. There was no service scheduled but he walked straight in with me right on his hammer.

Now, here's a church for you. The whole place is a crypt, so you have to creep around a bit. All the tombs come with a sculptured likeness of the occupant on the outside. Most of the folks are leaning on one elbow and seem ready for a bit of gossip. I wonder what they would have made of the latest news. As you might expect, there was an ethereal feel about the place and those in tourist mode were whispering amongst themselves. Anything louder would have been swept away as an eerie echo, as was soon made apparent.

My mark was seated in one of the front pews, silent and serene. From the side vestry, the muted resonance of a patriotic anthem was emerging. The sound intensified and soon there was no doubt. Someone was whistling *La Marseillaise* and I could tell that it was a female whistler. Don't ask me how I know these things. I just do.

Few countries do patriotism better than France. Napoleon's tomb is a big tribute to a little guy and the stature of the Maid D'Orleans is etched in gold with diffused arc lights for night viewing. You have to love a nation that pays homage to its heroes in such a way. They even have the gall to place a memorial to their lanky general up front and center. I mean, after all, wasn't he all piss and wind? Well, he is now, if the pigeons are any guide.

The whistler finally entered into the body of the church and headed for the front pew. Was she a female verger or only dressed like one? What would be said if I tried to disrobe her in the church? I decided to delay the denouement and just as well. With a squeal of delight, she embraced the young man in the front row. They looked at each other and embraced again. Don't you just hate family reunions?

"Hi Hank. How are you? You look terrific."

"So do you, Sis. Just look at you in your verger's robes. The folks in Choctaw, Mississippi aren't going to believe this."

Oh crap! Can you believe it? Harriet Hayseed reunites with Hank the Yank in the City of Light and Paddy Pest has just laid another egg. I didn't wait around to see what was in her brother's cylindrical package – probably some home-made grits from her mammy's country kitchen.

There are a lot of parks and squares around Paris and, once again, I was back to square one. It was a lonely place. Monsieur du Pleb from the insurance company had been on the blower and was making impatient noises.

"Monsieur Pest! L'heure tourne – the clock is ticking. Do you 'ave a suspect?"

I assured him that an arrest was imminent. I then purged my soul for once more gilding the lily and departed urgently for my evening tipple. If I miss happy hour, I'm in a bad mood for the rest of the evening.

You can't always be sure of a friendly ear when you are in a foreign drinking establishment and, quite often, people move to another table if you are objectionable. For this reason I often take along some reading material. I thoroughly recommend Dale Carnegie's classic best seller *How to Solve Crimes and Earn Brownie Points*. This was the right time to revisit one of his pertinent declarations: *When confusion arises, always return to the scene of the crime.*

The security people let me into the museum after closing time and, there I was, one-on-one with a perfect forgery of *La Ciaconda*. There was so much that I knew about the Mona Lisa but no more than the rest of the world. The lady was born in Florence and married there. She sat for Leonardo da Vinci and if she maintained any other bodily position, this would be pure conjecture. We do know that her favorite singer was Nat King Cole.

Da Vinci was quite an artist. No matter where you stand, the eyes of Mona Lisa seem to follow you and that waspish smile just melts your heart. I actually stood on my head and looked at her through my legs. I feel a bit reticent about saying this but her smile seemed to broaden. Perhaps because all of my money fell out of my pocket.

If you are an avid viewer of those television stories from the CSI franchise, you will be familiar with that instrument that highlights blood splatter. You just put on your goggles, turn out the lights and you've discovered the scene of the crime. I can't afford one of those units but I do have an earlier prototype that seeks out beer stains. It was a Christmas present from my dry-cleaner. I guess it was with hope rather than confidence that I scanned the oil painting and, therefore, the result was a revelation. The base of the painting was stained with beer, alright: Guinness beer.

So, there we have it. Not so much an American perpetrator but an Irish one. It certainly made my job a lot easier.

My Irish snitch in Paris was Jerry O'Shaughnessy. He would be hovering over a pint somewhere and I knew that there was an Irish pub not far from the River Seine. I waited under a nearby bridge. And waited! Eventually, the bells of Notre Dame pealed long and loud. The ghost of Quasimodo must have licked his lips in anticipation of cool refreshing ale. It was five o'clock.

There was no mistaking the slightly hunched figured that limped forward in the shadow of his cloth cap and a thousand misdemeanors. Jerry had no official means of support but he always managed to acquire enough of the readies to keep him in the manner to which he was accustomed.

There was little that managed to get past this Hibernian vagabond that couldn't be on-sold for a hard cash payment.

I slipstreamed into the pub on his coat-tails and the perfunctory greeting was followed by the release of my credit card to the man behind the bar. I was hoping that Jerry wasn't in one of his drinking moods. I had previously tried to keep up with him on his marathon booze sessions and had finished the worse for wear.

"It's been a long time, Jerry. How might you be?"

"Not too bad, Paddy. Not too bad, at all. What would you be doing out on such a soft day?"

To tell you the truth, I was so deep in thought; I hardly noticed that it had been raining. I told him what had gone down and the news of the theft didn't seem to surprise. He wasn't quick to blame the IRA, which was usually the case. Anyway, they would have done the deed on Saint Patrick's Day. There was a lot of mumbling and he made a few phone calls before he became seriously thirsty and I had to top up his tipple. This is always an exact science for interrogators who need to loosen the tongue without providing an over-supply of product. In the end, I got what I wanted and left him there with a hot toddy. The next morning I was on the plane to Dublin.

Jerry O'Shaughnessy

Ireland in general and Dublin in particular have been on a bit of a roller-coaster ride over the past century. The locals have had to contend with a potato famine, insurrection, home-rule, civil war, religious tension and, most recently, financial distress. It has been enough to wipe the smile off everyone's face. Nevertheless, this is no excuse – Sean O'Gorman should never have stolen the Mona Lisa.

O'Gorman and his wife ran a small framing and poster business in Fleet Street and they were hit by the financial collapse more than most. Dubliners were going to the wall, left, right and center and people were more interested in hanging their bank managers, rather than iconic images. Enter Dario da Vinci, an Italian entrepreneur and agent. He was doing some scouting prior to the forthcoming tour of his client, the rock band, Stromboli Sunrise. If Sean could get his act together in three weeks, he had the contract for five thousand posters, to be distributed all over Ireland, with payment on completion of the project.

You know how these things go. The lead singer of Stromboli Sunrise overdosed on cocaine in a Palermo night club and the tour was cancelled. Da Vinci was never seen again and O'Gorman was left with five thousand posters, cash on delivery.

Irish people are not renowned for dispensing curses but Sean O'Gorman certainly laid one on the da Vinci family and sought retribution. I have to say that this was a little unfair as there was no way that Dario's real name was da Vinci. He was an opportunist and these kinds of people do things like that. Nevertheless, Sean reckoned that he was owed big time and that was his motivation to plunder what he thought was rightfully his.

"I'll get that feckin' wop bastard" screamed the felonious fellow from Fleet St as they led him away. I thought that he was very lucky to get away with his life as I could see *the Froggies* dusting off their guillotine. In the end, they seized his forgery and hung it in his jail cell, so he would never forget what he had done.

Naturally, I was lauded for my investigative work and the whole thing was hushed up to such an extent that hardly anybody ever heard about it. I was half expecting to be awarded the Legion of Honor or a Croix de Guerre but there wasn't a convenient war on at the time. I settled for dinner with the French President and his wife at the Élysée Palace and, I have to say, the First Lady is some good-looking chicky babe.

I would have liked to have been closer to the gorgeous creature but you know how those long tables are. They are built to seat forty people and there were only three of us. She had deep penetrating eyes and I don't think she took them off me all night. And that waspish smile! Now, where have I seen that before?

PEST TAKES A CHANCE

The Casino de Monte Carlo is everything that you would want it to be. The ornate Belle Époque facade promises much and delivers in spades. They also have hearts, diamonds and clubs in most rooms. I do like a game of chance and such a place is always a magnetic attraction, when I roll into town.

"Bon Soir, Monsieur Pest. We are 'appy to see you, again. Perhaps, you have the luck, this time." Need I say that their eyes lit up every time they saw me? I have never been a lucky gambler.

I can vividly remember the first time I came to Monaco. I hooked up with a lady called Grace. She was a real charmer. *Chemin de Fer* was her specialty and she arranged my entry into the Salon Privé, where this card game is played for high stakes. The first few times I won and she thought that I was the bee's knees. Yes, she was married but had some kind of loose arrangement with her husband. He must have been a real prince.

Grace Mourakakis wasn't totally honest about her connubial situation. Her husband was a wealthy mobster from Athens and the arrangement was all in his favor. He ran a string of good-time floozies but was extremely jealous if Grace ever found solace in the arms of somebody else. So, I got banged up a bit. Still, it's nice to have these fond memories.

Paddy Pest has always been on good terms with the French Sûreté, the national police force. They often call me in when they need help. I have a good track record on their turf. These little jobs also give me the opportunity to take home some duty-free foie gras or truffles, which I flog to some of our up-market restaurants for an unbelievable price.

The word was out that something big was going down in the casino that night. My Gallic friends had given me a substantial cash advance with instruction to act naturally. So, I started out by leering lasciviously at all the exquisite crumpet that I could see. I do that quite well. The Grand Prix circus was in town and the casino was buzzing. The babes were frocked-up and there was money to burn. I wondered if I could turn my small fortune into a large fortune. I set up camp at one of the craps tables.

Craps is a totally confusing dice game. It even has its own language, which is modified over time in a tribute to the ever-changing vernacular of the day. All you need to know is that a double one is *snake eyes* and *up pops the devil* if you throw a seven. Some of you will be familiar with the craps shoot from that evergreen musical *Guys and Dolls*. The Big Palooka managed to win all the money because he used his own dice. Is this why the dealer was looking so confident?

I never managed to find out. The sound of a loud whip crack was followed by the devastating sight of their most imposing chandelier crashing to the floor. The lights went out and the security alarms started whining. There was pandemonium. Some quick-thinking patrons tried to make it to the exits but the doors were closed. I patted my under-arm Beretta and also snaked my hand over the immediate vicinity of the table, in case there were some unclaimed chips available. It was then that the calm voice of reason wafted through the room, amplified by some kind of portable loud-speaker.

"We only want your valuables. You will not be harmed."

This quite reasonable solicitation was greeted with screams and cries of anguish and a number of ladies fainted. However, one prima donna went on and on. Her decibel ceiling was quite intolerable. A shot rang out and the screaming stopped.

The bad guy again! "I should mention that I do have a low tolerance to noise."

The room fell silent and the thieves went about their business. They must have been wearing night-vision glasses because the house lights remained off. Their path around the tables was punctuated by stifles and screams as necklaces' were ripped from necks and wallets were removed from jackets and man-bags.

I have to say that that the voice of their spokesman sounded familiar. I wondered if he might have worked for the Olympic movement because every announcement was made in English, French and Esperanto. Perhaps he was a citizen of the Hutt River Province in Western Australia: one of the few places that still rates Esperanto as a language. My suspicions were further enhanced when one of the scoundrels not only cashed me out but also helped himself to my Beretta. "Bewdy mate."

Now, where have I heard an accent like that, before?

The culprits disappeared as fast as they had arrived. I heard the sound of a few turbo-charged engines and I wondered if Bernie Ecclestone (the Formula One Chief) might have been involved. Then again, he doesn't need the money.

Of course, there were repercussions at the Palace. This was an embarrassment for the principality and the security service at the casino was hauled over the coals in no uncertain manner. I wasn't feeling too good myself but I knew that my job wasn't over. I had leads and who knew where they would take me? But, first things first! You can't start anything in France before breakfast. Certainly, I couldn't start my car. Flat battery! As I said, I had leads and it wasn't long before I was on the road again.

Le Grand Pain is not the hangover that it seems. This is a chain of bakeries and pâtisseries where you can get baguettes, croissants and all kinds of jam infested succulents by the hour. I needed an hour to contemplate my next move and pulled into their small café on the road to Nice. It appeared that they were having a run of Australian customers. My predecessors were described as loud, jocular and elegantly dressed fellows. They were all wearing diamond necklaces and ear-rings. The proprietor thought nothing of it – probably just the latest trend.

So, there it was. My compatriots were the villains and I wondered if they were permanently based in Europe or just on a busman's holiday. Did they have the contacts to dispose of the jewels? Australia is a big country and we have a lot of fences but these lads were looking for someone special. I had a few contacts in dark places, so I quickly polished off my *petit dejeuner* and headed west. Nice was nice but I needed to be in Marseille. I arrived just in time for lunch.

Because Marseille is a port town, it is an obvious place to try the bouillabaisse and as far as fish soup goes, there is none better. You always get a nice drop of red wine to compliment your main selection and so I settled in for the afternoon. Dark places don't become illuminated until after dark and I knew that my man liked to work in the shadows.

The fence that I looked up was in a bit of a predicament. We were tight but he had other obligations and there were customers who relied on his discretion. That's the way it is in that business. I was forced to shell out for a twenty-year old bottle of Châteauneuf du Pape. It was just the right tipple to loosen his tongue although it did take some time. There was a half-decent chop house just down the road. We plundered the menu, finishing with Calvados and coffee. By then, he was bursting to tell me all and I was extremely grateful.

"Paddy, the loot has been assessed. Much of it is fake."

"You must be joking." I stammered. "Are you serious?"

"Totally!"

I had to laugh. No wonder some of those dames in the casino didn't bother screaming.

The important thing for me was to get a name and then the dominos would fall into place. I had time on my side as payment had not yet occurred. The crooks would still be in the country and that gave me a chance. What more can you ask?

When you've got time on your side in Marseille, it is always good to appreciate the artistic temperament of the city. There has been so much written and said about the tough and gruff history of the waterfront that sometimes the gentle aspects of this town are overlooked. The arts community is huge and galleries and other cultural opportunities are there for all to see. In fact, I felt quite ashamed that I spent most of the night in a strip club. Bad habits die hard.

They hire a lot of Australian girls at the Lido and places like that because you have to have long legs and be six feet tall. I would imagine that if you are six feet tall, you've probably got long legs, anyway. Priscilla got her start at the Moulin Rouge and, in those days, she was probably a red-head. There have been quite a few bottle rinses since then but in the twilight of her career she blended in beautifully with the lobster and prawns of Marseille. The vegetables who sat in the cheap seats were appreciative, also.

I'm not going to tell you how I came by this lead but you can't beat the power of positive thinking. If there are Aussie blokes about, a beaut sheila will not be far away. Naturally, I invited her to my table and we shared a bottle of vin ordinaire. It was so ordinary, I nearly threw up.

Listening to Priscilla's life story was enough to put me on suicide watch. I asked her to gloss over the details of her tawdry youth and to share her recent conquests with me.

"Anyone who speaks Esperanto?"

As it happens, she had recently fallen for a guy from Western Australia.

"Get out of here," I exclaimed. When she took me literally, I had to chase her and bring her back to the table. She was now crying.

I like to think that I am a bit of a metrosexual kind of a guy. I am actually not quite sure what that means but it does sound appropriate in France. Evidently, we can't walk past a *Banana Republic* store without making a purchase. I don't know about that but I do know that I am uncomfortable when women hit the water-works button. To make matters worse, all the other patrons thought that I was responsible for the lady's distress. There was booing and hissing.

The real cause of her distress was the fact that Mr Wonderful was leaving town in a couple of days. I could only share her distress and suggested that we get together on a double date. She thought that this was a great idea and looked forward to meeting my Miss Wonderful, who would be a policewoman in disguise.

I don't think that Lucinda Le Bras had ever been on a major bust before, not that she wasn't a major bust herself. I don't know how she fitted into her uniform. When I told her that she would have to dispense with the official gear, she seemed quite pleased and even more so when I instructed her to show affection whenever possible. Priscilla's man was called Ron and even he was taken aback with the enthusiastic fervor of her greeting. I think that all Australians are a little bemused by the multiple kisses that emanate as part of the Gallic salutation. We never have enough cheeks.

Ron was a nice enough chap but he was pretty tight-lipped. I tried to be discreet as I searched for any tell-tale signs that he had been wearing jewelry. There was no bulge where my Beretta might be. He said that he had a pest eradication business. Yours truly gulped rather alarmingly but I was pretty sure that he had no idea of my surname. I countered with an equally ridiculous occupation: a private eye-surgeon. We chewed the fat for a while and tried to bring Lucinda into the conversation but her English was not that good. However, she was breathing and we both enjoyed that.

I tried to get Ron pissed in order that he might let down his guard but this dude was a cool customer. I was hoping that Priscilla might be given a farewell gift of a diamond tiara or something like that but it never happened. At least, we had the restaurant staked out and the boys in blue would certainly follow him home. We needed to establish his whereabouts at all times and, in due course, the whereabouts of his buddies.

The tail worked a treat and, the following day, we isolated four co-conspirators. However, I could have kicked myself. They are Australians. Where else would they be but on their surf boards?

"Monsieur Pest! Elles sont sur La Plage. We 'ave them under observation."

I instructed Le Bras to paddle out to the breaking waves and make contact. I figured that when they saw her in her bikini, they would probably give themselves up. I was wrong. They tipped the floating femme into the water and headed out to sea. In the distance, I saw irascible Ron rounding the headland in a jet-boat. Damn! He had given the gendarmes the slip. It wouldn't be long before he rescued his mates. I didn't have a moment to lose. It was obvious that Lucy was not a good swimmer but I would have to leave her in the bubbling undercurrent for an hour or so. She did have good buoyancy.

The coast guard and the air-wing were both alerted and we hired two dolphins from Brigitte Bardot's animal farm. Dolphins are very good at following people and we attached transmitters to the fish. We were obliged to MI Cinq for their involvement.

The Aussie raiders made landfall at a place called Méjean and we were waiting for them. There was a fire fight and things got pretty tense for a while. In fact, it was like the finale to a James Bond movie: explosions, confusion and the victory of good over evil.

As is the want of heroes, I singled out the gang leader. Ron tried to run but he couldn't hide. I caught up with him on the cliff face and we struggled as only two Australians can. Some people said that I pushed him over the edge but this was not so. He slipped. I tried to grab him but I only managed to retrieve my Beretta. He was certainly my next priority but things happened too quickly. The Esperanto Kid crashed to the rocks below and was so smashed-up his mother wouldn't have recognized him. At first, the other felons played dumb and maintained that they thought we were chasing them because of a water speed violation. After two hours in a small room with skilled interrogators, who were breathing garlic down their neck, they confessed.

The stolen valuables were all recovered and half a dozen wholesale jewelers went out of business in Marseille. My friend was chuffed because he would no longer have any competition. It certainly pays to have an ally like Paddy Pest.

I personally returned the booty to the casino and they rewarded me with some gratuitous gambling chips – quite a few, actually. I made my way to my favorite spot at the craps table and eye-balled the wily devil that would try and recover them for the house.

Not today, bon ami! I was feeling lucky.

ONE MORE CHANCE

Linda entered the room wearing one of those Teddy things. She had nice legs, a waist to die for and there was a small tattoo above her left breast. The gun that was aimed at me was a snub-nosed colt thirty-eight. Obviously, she was not going to believe that I was a Seventh Day Adventist.

There had been a screen door but the main entrance was open. A voice from the back of the house provided an invitation.

"Come on in. I won't be long."

In fact, she was long. Lean, too! There was definite muscle tone on her arms and those fluffy slippers didn't detract from her menacing appearance. In my business you meet a lot of tough dames. Life has not dealt them a winning hand and they like to take it out on the opposite sex. I wondered if I should have worn a dress. The lady came right to the point.

"Who are you? What do you want?"

My opening gambit was "Hi Babe. How are they hanging?"

I sometimes use this downtown jive talk in order to put people at ease and in this instance it worked. She lowered her gun and liberated a cigarette from a packet on the table. She didn't offer me one. Nor did her eyes ever leave mine. I can't tell you how horny I was starting to feel.

Linda Mustardo was well known to the vice squad in three states but had never been involved in any nefarious activities that could be construed as life threatening. If she knew how to use that gun, there were probably no live witnesses to testify to the fact. I introduced myself and it was a little self-deflating to learn that she had never heard of Paddy Pest.

"Are you with the Irish mafia?" she asked in all innocence.

I told her that I was looking for Flatface Freddy O'Flaherty and was under the impression that he lived at this address. "He does, sometimes," purred the tall blonde, who was now becoming more congenial. She rubbed her delicate fingers up the lapel of my finely worsted Armani jacket. "What's your interest, lover-boy?"

I hadn't been called lover-boy for over a week so you can imagine that I was captivated by the attention of one so lovely. Freddy owed me money but I didn't want to paint myself as a debt-collector. It would reduce the sheen of my otherwise sophisticated polish. Should the truth be known, he probably owed her money as well.

The doll readily accepted that this was just a social visit and offered me a drink. I could see where this was going and I figured that if we made it to the bedroom, I could rifle some of Freddy's pockets. His clothes would surely be hanging in her closet. You may think that this is the act of a desperate man but the fact was that I had a big tip for a long-shot in the last race at Sandown. Right there and then I was tapped out.

They say that gin is an aphrodisiac and I can believe that. We were in the bedroom before you could say *London Dry* and our timing was most fortuitous. Before I had even loosened my tie, there was an almighty explosion and the front window of the sitting room imploded. A petrol bomb!

Flames took hold of the drapes and the bar disintegrated in the wake of excessive alcohol. Smoke poured out through every outlet and it wasn't long before the sirens of the fire trucks alerted us to the fact that the neighbors had been vigilant. The police wouldn't be far behind and this fact had Linda on tender hooks. She palmed-off the gun to me and asked if I would stash it somewhere. Who's the bunny, then?

I don't know why I decided that the under-side of the mattress might be a good hiding spot. It was so obvious. It turned out to be the happiest moment of my life. Under the mattress was a substantial pile of hundred dollar bills, all bundled up and cash-ready for a spendthrift with a sense of humor. This would be me. There must have been ten grand, there. It would have been a bonanza for the housekeeper but Paddy got there first. It seemed a fair exchange for the firearm that I left in its place.

In what was left of the main room, the forensic team had discovered the remains of an uncouth message to Freddy. It was definitely Flatface that they were after, rather than Linda or yours truly. This would not have been much consolation if we had dallied with the foreplay. Fortunately, I do have an uncanny ability to make my moves at the right time. I decided that it would be a good time to move as far away from this place as possible and I made my excuses to the lady of the house. The arson squad didn't see me slip away through a side entrance.

"If it isn't Paddy Pest. Hey Paddy, come and bet with me. You know you want to."

The bookmakers were delighted to see me at the track. They always are. Admittedly, I arrived with only three races left on the card but I was thrilled to discover that my gun bet was still at long odds. For those of you who are ignorant as to the ways and means of price calculation, I can tell you that a fifty-to-one chance is an animal that has been proven to have limited speed or stamina and has earned a reputation for consistently being a late arrival. There are only two solutions to this problem. You give the horse a stimulating additive to make it run faster or you give the opposing steeds something to make them run more slowly.

I had no idea which option my guys were taking but something was up. The trainer was keeping a low profile and so was the jock, usually an unstoppable chatterbox. The horse seemed to have something on his mind but the strapper's interpretive skills were questionable. There was nothing but optimism, there.

I was nervous. There were too many people hovering around the connections. I certainly didn't like the way that the Chief Steward was looking at the animal.

What can you say about the Chief Steward? At a time when we are all looking for admirable role-models in the sporting arena, we could do no better than point our career-minded youngsters in this direction. As far as adjudicators are concerned, it is far less dangerous than being a football umpire and the torrent of abuse, will, for the most part, come from people who are smaller than you.

Stewards also possess wide-ranging powers that can be instigated before and after a race. They even have the authority to delay or cancel proposed dividend payments. Can you believe that? My money was already on and the inquisitive fellow was looking the horse in the eye and smelling his breath. My God! Surely, this is one orifice that is sacrosanct?

Jeopardy made it to the barrier, alright and when the gates opened, he departed the stalls at speed. In fact, he was jumping out of his skin. Although the jockey tried to restrain him, the animal immediately raced to the front of the pack. All around me, the punters were stunned; even more so when he bounded into the straight and won by six lengths. The hoop still couldn't restrain him and the animal continued his gallop for another mile. Oh dear!

Things then got rather unpleasant. On return to the enclosure, horse and jockey were abused. Above the jeers and catcalls, I heard the words "elephant juice" mentioned a number of times. There were going to be repercussions and the strapper's attempt to spirit the horse away before he could be swabbed was farcical, to say the least. Connections were hauled before the stewards, although this process was delayed. The rider was in the medical room, where they were calling him Mr Monkey. Both of his arms had been stretched six inches.

Suspensions were handed out all around and the horse was disqualified. There would be no payout. If this wasn't bad enough, can you imagine how I felt when I heard that they had arrested Flatface Freddy O'Flaherty? I expect that jail was probably the safest place for Freddy as it appeared that there were people out to get him. However, when he discovered that his bail money was short by ten grand, he would not be pleased. In truth, should I have received my rightful dividend, I had every intention of returning the borrowed funds to their hiding place. It would also have given me an excuse to revisit a very lovely lady.

Then again, as Freddy was banged up, I went around there, anyway.

THE CLINIC

You meet a lot of interesting people in a drug and alcohol rehabilitation clinic: mostly entertainers, nannies and divorcees with multiple convictions. Their life experience is far more exciting than the average urban drone and I always like to isolate and analyze those who might have a particularly interesting story to tell. At the Holy Hell Rehabilitation Center, there were three such individuals: the Sudanese refugee, the Sri Lankan singer and a Wonga Wingi elder. The Wonga Wingi was an aboriginal tribe of nomads who had moved on and left Yakedy Do behind. What a strange name. I must ask him about it, one day.

I mention these three people because any one of them would have been an obvious target for a vindictive villain, especially Jamal, the Sri Lankan singer. His version of *Moon River* was an on-going highlight at the monthly tea-dance but the fact that he continually maintained the lyrical onslaught during his morning ablutions did not go down well with the rest of his house-mates. I think that this might be fair warning to others who sing in the shower: people who are completely unaware of the wrath of irritation that simmers beyond the bath-room door.

In the end, it was poor Jessie Thistlewaite who was murdered but I don't know why. She was a very friendly soul and not an unattractive woman for her age. For a while, Paddy Pest was in the gun but I was able to explain that my nocturnal visits to her cottage were mostly due to sleep-walking.

The surrounds of the Holy Hell Rehabilitation Center were quite extensive. A number of small cottages provided accommodation facilities away from the main mansion and the gardens were a tribute to the various ground-keepers. These gentlemen kept everything looking peachy. Now they were under the microscope.

"I want you to down your tools and congregate in the main house," said the policeman.

They grudgingly obeyed his command but they were not happy. The shrubs needed watering and there were petunias to plant. When they got to the main house, it was just like one of those Agatha Christie novels. All the residents and staff were herded into the drawing room and the Chief Inspector announced that Jessie had been killed by a rake. Everybody turned and looked at me. In point of fact, she had been killed by a garden rake. Right through the left eye would you believe?

Some of this might sound familiar. When I signed in on my first day, the English matron said that I would love it there. It was just like Midsomer in the old country. Who hasn't had to sweep countless bodies out of their television set after watching an episode of this British pot-boiler? I wondered how many of us would make it through the night.

The nights are never easy. If the demons come, they do not tread lightly. If you scream, you get carted off to a sealed unit and are fitted with a complimentary straight jacket. Then, they give you prune juice for breakfast. The ignominy of it all! Perhaps Jessie is in a better place.

Inspector Plod was aware of my credentials and it was only a matter of time before he would seek my counsel or so I thought. That loony harridan, Hilary Huckmeister, complicated matters when she screamed out at the top of her voice "He did it. He did it. There's the lousy bastard who did it." She sounded like a parrot I once knew.

Once again, everybody looked at me. Of course, most of the residents were aware that Hilary could be a difficult woman if she wasn't taking her medication and methinks that she had also spiked her cough syrup. This was an old trick amongst professional imbibers and who was I to be critical?

"Now Hilary, settle down. You have a fanciful imagination and it is getting the better of you." She glared at me with complete disdain. A chill went down my spine.

The gentleman in charge was no Hercule Poirot but he wasn't a bad sort of a chap. He noted the witch's comments and dismissed the others with the warning that they shouldn't leave town. He needn't have worried. Scaling Colditz Castle would have been an easier task. Surprisingly, I was invited over to the murder scene: the cottage of heavenly flowers. Each of the cottages had equally ridiculous names but none of them had a tool shed. The central depositary for all garden implements was situated in a dark corner of the estate near one of the smaller flower plots and just thirty meters from Jessie's residence. When we arrived, the rake was still sticking out of her head.

They call this kind of thing blunt force trauma and I am more of an expert on penetrating trauma, which is usually down to bullets – not that those metal prongs didn't leave their mark. Laying there with all that dried blood over her mouth, she looked like a one-eyed Purple People Eater. I didn't like to say anything in case somebody thought that it was in bad taste but it was a catchy song. Nobody noticed me whistling the melody.

Forensics is important at all murder scenes. While the people in boiler suits bagged and tagged everything, I nosed around the room. Holy Hell was not a cheap ride but they gave you value for money. The three bedroom bungalow was decked out in provincial country cottage style and the furnishings were rudimentary but comfortable. Jessie's fellow residents had remained at the big house: Rebecca O'Rourke and the harlot, Hilary Huckmeister. They both appeared to be suitably shocked.

I was keen to get into the victim's bedroom before the forensics crew but this was proving difficult. Inspector Plod was sticking to me like a leech but I needn't have worried. They did find a packet of Wally Golightly condoms in her top drawer but nothing to connect her with me. I let out an audible sigh and felt confident that they would never discover that we knew each other from my New York days. We often had breakfast at Ziffany's.

Yes, Jessie Thistlewaite was an American and I know that you wouldn't think so with a name like that. She was very much part of this nefarious business that I am in. If you thought that I wasn't grieving, you would be wrong. The lady was very close to me and also to others – I often used her in a honey trap in order to turn a prospective informant. Through my tutelage, she learned to have sex in six languages.

Jessie Thistlewaite: rest in peace

It was a shame about the drink. It always gets you in the end. We both burned the candle at both ends and I thought that she would find salvation in Australia. This is a great country: beaches, babes and beautiful sunshine. However, the men are all turds like me and she hooked up with a few bad apples. Jessie finally found salvation at the bottom of a whisky glass. I booked into Holy Hell to cover her ass, so to speak.

"Well, Jessie! You're going to be out of here in a few weeks. How do you feel about the booze, now?"

"I feel thirsty, Paddy, but I think I can handle it. I'm more worried about you. When did they tell you that you were beyond redemption?"

This was the last conversation I had with my American friend and I owed it to her to try and solve the crime. To my mind, there were two obvious suspects. You probably know where I am going with this. Hilary Huckmeister was not only a harlot and a harridan but a horrible, horny hump-bunny. She played for both teams and I reckon she had the hots for Jessie: a passionate overture that was probably rejected. The Sudanese refugee was the other person who had aroused my suspicions. Slapdash was a bit of a loudmouth and he always said what he thought. Sometimes it would have been better if he didn't think at all.

I expect that this guy somehow slipped through the immigration net. He was a monster of a man and I couldn't really see him as a victim of persecution. Thistlewaite had been to Sudan and I wonder if she recognized him for what he really was. Jamal was a different story. He didn't need to kill Jessie – another singing appearance at the tea-dance and she would have committed suicide.

There was one final member on my short list of prospective killers. Quite frankly, I just didn't know what to think of Yakedy Do. For a start, he talked such gibberish. I had no idea what he was going on about and I shudder to think what he was like when he was drinking. However, unless the lady was taking didgeridoo lessons from him, I could see no obvious link, which is essential in order to prosecute a case. As I glanced down at the prostrate corpse with the rake still attached to her cranium, I noticed a rather guilty looking gardener standing nearby. Could the answer to this complex murder be simplicity in the extreme? Had she made a disparaging remark about the roses and suffered the ultimate consequence?

I don't think that we will ever know. The dinner bell rang and everyone dashed off to the dining room for the Friday swill. It was meatloaf followed by a chunky custard dessert. My favorite! The only downside was that in the absence of Jessie Thistlewaite, I had to sit next to that hopeless horn-bag, Hilary Huckmeister.

There was no way that I was going to cover her ass.

Pest in his New York days

–4–

TRANSITION

Although some of these stories have a religious bent, evolution is not just a philosophical phenomenon. A simple change of job, an ambitious determination or an ounce of luck can all be motivation enough to change one's circumstances. Of course, not always for the better.

My store of heroes is fast running out and so I leave you with a gaggle of ordinary folks who have done extraordinary things, mostly for their own benefit. It is difficult to ascertain where your sympathies may lie with this lot but I can give you some good news – we've got a Paddy-free run from here on in.

HOLY ORDERS

Virginia Kilpatrick and I go back a long way. Together, we won the wheelbarrow race at the Warringal Park Fair in a cakewalk. Some said that we shouldn't have been in it because we were teenagers and the other contestants were only six and seven. Isn't jealousy a curse? On reflection, I think that I was probably the last person for Ginny to open her legs for. Not long after that, she went into the convent.

People said that it was surprising that we weren't an item because we had so much in common. Our opinions were the same on just about everything and we shared the same kind of black humor. I can remember when I put a harmless tree snake into Miss Chalker's lunch box and she laughed her head off, Virginia, that is. Miss Chalker actually had a heart attack and was rushed to hospital. We had to get a new teacher and in mid-term, too.

When Ginny left for the nunnery and started her new life as a novitiate, I used to try and get down there as often as possible. We passed the time by walking through their beautiful gardens and there was hardly anything that she wouldn't tell me. I gathered that all was not well with her and the Mother Superior, who was a bit of a tyrant. My friend was disappointed when I told her that she was not living in a good area for tree snakes.

It was some months later when I heard the tragic news that they had found the same Reverend Mother in the bell tower, hanging from her bootstraps. There was much speculation but none of the explanations rang true. Strangely, the coroner found that she died by misadventure, whatever that means. The convent was rocked with another scandal just before Christmas when it was discovered that her replacement, who was also a bit of a disciplinarian, had been poisoned. Her habits were regular and it appears that someone had tampered with her hot nourishing broth, which she always enjoyed before retiring for the night. The police interviewed Sister Virginia but she claimed that she alone prepared the beverage and no-one could have interfered. She was such a sweet young person, they didn't even consider not believing her.

It is often said that tragedies come in threes but I don't think that anyone could have foreseen what actually happened next. A reporter from the local news service put it into perspective.

"This is Gunter Snufflebum from the Channel Nine news and we are witnessing the biggest blaze in these parts for many a year. Our Lady of Good Luck convent has just had some bad luck. The whole place has burnt down."

In those days, Guy Fawkes Night was always celebrated with a bonfire and all the kids from the neighborhood would gather around and throw things on the fire: effigies, school books and all that kind of stuff. It was an ill wind that blew that night. Some of the embers were swept into the tool shed, where there was an open can of lawn mower fuel. The shed exploded and the fire took control in minutes.

Despite the best efforts of the bucket brigade, the heritage buildings were destroyed and there was only rubble left to inspect. It didn't make it into the press but it is rumored that the investigators found gunpowder residue and started asking questions. Ginny was able to explain to them that the kitchen always made egg, curry and gunpowder sandwiches on Monday and this explanation was accepted. Such a lovely girl! Why bother asking anyone else?

After all this, we lost contact for a while but it didn't surprise me to learn that the novitiate had left holy orders and tried to make it in the real world. She was quite proficient on the guitar and had a passable singing voice. Although Virginia was a finalist on *Religious Idol*, the singing nun thing had been done before and went nowhere. For a while, she was fronting an arts program on the television but this didn't last either. Nobody knew what she was talking about. I then heard that the convent cutie had taken on a job as a bookie's clerk. The lass was good with figures and was a quick learner. In less than twelve months, she applied for a wagering license and subsequently became the state's only female bookmaker.

Although there are a few women in the industry these days, back then it was outrageous and some of her peers found it hard to take her seriously. She had strident arguments with them all but none more so than with Lou

Surfa, who also happened to be the bookmaker's advisory chief. I think that there might also have been a bit of sexual harassment there, as well.

They found Lou's body in the day yard of one of the local stables. He had had an altercation with a horse's hoof. The indelible imprint from the metal shoe was well defined on his fractured cranium. In some cases this is not a terminal injury but in this instance it was. The authorities were disappointed that Lou had left the bookmaker's ring because he always gave the best odds but horses can be dangerous to be around. Just as the investigators were about to close the case, somebody noticed that his pecker had been cut off.

As you might expect, all the other bookies were interrogated in the hope that someone might know if anybody had it in for Lou. There was one body that immediately came to mind but that box-cutter that Ginny always kept in her top pocket was obviously a major deterrent. I wonder why nobody ever asked her about that.

As you might be aware, I spend a large part of my life at the track, so it was inevitable that our paths would cross. At first, she didn't recognize me due to the ravages of time. We then managed some private moments, together and I was able to introduce her to some on-course associates of mine.

"If I was you, Ginny," I said. "I wouldn't get too close to these people. Just get close to their money." I don't think that she was listening.

For some reason, she seemed to hit it off with a weasel named Patrick Johncock, aka Pat the Prick. Johncock was a stand-over man, drug dealer and shyster. As he was always pretty cashed-up, Ginny took him on as a client and was doing quite well out of it because he rarely placed a winning wager. But he was such a low-life. I don't know how she maintained her composure. Johncock liked to think that he was a bit of a ladies' man and preferred girls with big boobs. Sometimes he used to place huge bets on the bottom weight so Ginny would have to bend down to wind-back the price.

Unfortunately, he was also a dangerous man with a quick temper and his handiwork was often on show. His appearances on the red carpet for football award nights were often controversial. If his escort didn't arrive swathed in bandages, she was likely wearing an eye patch or limping through the event on crutches.

The announcement of their proposed nuptials was greeted with absolute disbelief throughout the racing community and I, for one, strenuously attempted to dissuade her from this life-defining commitment. Nevertheless, she was confident that she could make him change his ways. Remarkably, his whole demeanor changed within weeks of their engagement. In fact, he sometimes seemed to cower in her presence and as the date of the wedding became increasingly imminent, he seemed to become more nervous.

Everybody laughed at the fact that Patrick was marrying a Kilpatrick, well, everyone except Pat. With what he had learned over the period of their courtship, he was prepared to take six to four that he wouldn't last nine months. Ginny's bookmaker friends were offering even money that he wouldn't make the New Year. He actually lasted two years.

I can't think of anything more painful than dying in an acid bath but, really, what was Pat thinking? Virginia explained to the police that she had prepared the acid pool in order to rejuvenate the candelabra, porcelain and other rusted object d'art that the lady of the house had, sadly, failed to maintain on a continual basis. She was not one for menial housework. At the last moment, Ginny had been called away to the local gambling club (she was a co-owner) where there had been an unprecedented run on one of the poker machines.

Patrick, who had been attending an elite sportsmen's night, chose that moment to arrive home. He was in a state of total inebriation and feeling rather chilly from the cold winter night. You can imagine how inviting that steaming hot bath must have looked when he pushed open the bathroom door.

"Thank you, Ginny. You've run a bath for me. How considerate!"

The coroner decided that it was a tragic misadventure and felt that Pat was decidedly unlucky because he somehow hit his head on the candelabra on the way into the bath. There were no fingerprints on the lighting fixtures, other than Ginny's, so foul play was not an issue.

I don't know whether Mrs Johncock-Kilpatrick had access to all her late husband's secret bank accounts but she certainly became more prominent socially and was a regular customer at the many designer boutiques around town. I am not sure what the required grieving time is for a weasel sleazebag but she completely ignored the fundamental tenets of mourning and started to party hard within minutes of the cremation. Incidentally, there was no Johncock family presence at the service. Evidently, they were all in jail.

The grieving widow!

People often marvel at those who amass huge fortunes and, certainly, there are those who are able to convert a turnip into a multi-national agricultural business. Most folks find marriage or inheritance an easier path to tread and so it was with Virginia. Pat's ill-gotten gains gave her the capital to expand and prosper and soon that small gambling club in the suburbs morphed into three casinos and a popular on-line betting facility. At Flemington, she was taking massive wagers from some heavy gamblers and was the undoubted leader of the rails bookmaking fraternity.

I am not sure whether her popularity was due to her personality or her notoriety but Virginia Kilpatrick (she had dumped her married name) was invited everywhere and she became a darling of the social set. Naturally, the lady was invited to the Governor's pony club gymkhana, which was held in the grounds of Government House every year. In fact, she sponsored one of the events and was asked to be a judge alongside the Premier. This was quite an honor.

The Premier, Richard "Call me Rick" O'Flannery was an Irish catholic who may well have had leprechauns in his family tree. He was lucky if he was five feet four inches tall. Nevertheless, he was full of blarney in a nice kind of way and Virginia was captivated. He was presently unmarried and there was even a rumor about that he was on the right side of fifty. However, I believe that he instigated that rumor himself.

Apart from her obvious charms, Virginia was of great interest to Rick because the gaming industry was responsible for keeping his government afloat. Without the industry's considerable turnover tax, they would be in deep trouble. The budget had already been blown on healthcare and education and now they were having huge problems with their transport infrastructure. So, what's new?

It is important for politicians to find stress relief away from the rigors of office and most lean on their family to provide a distraction; even if their particular unit is represented by a nagging wife and five screaming kids. The O'Flannery tribe had left the nest and his missus had run off with her Pilates instructor. I might add that the media had a field day with that one. The Pilates instructor was female.

I can't seem to recall when Rick and Virginia first started dating but I do know that there was some early subterfuge. He put together some hastily convened focus groups in order that their paths would cross. However, it wasn't long before it was accepted that they were in a relationship and she became an adornment on his arm at most social functions around town.

"Doesn't Rick's lady friend look so serene? I don't think that butter would melt in her mouth." This casual observer was about to be shocked. So was the dairy industry.

There was an expectation that they would eventually tie the knot but I can't remember any firm commitment being announced through the Department of Information. Being an election year, I would imagine that Rick had other things on his mind but if he had asked me, I would have advised that he didn't take his lady friend for granted. She is not the kind of person who likes to be ignored.

People started to notice a chill in their relationship about the time of the Moomba march (let's get together and have fun) but what did the man expect? You get hit with the same old political spin that he directs at his constituents and everything becomes unbelievably boring. Smart and snide remarks and offensive retorts creep into your conversations and both of you are flying off at the slightest provocation. It all came to a tragic end on one dark, moonless night in late November.

It was early evening on the day of the election and it looked like the result would be close. If the decision was down to postal votes, the counting would take a few days to process. Rick and Ginny decided to dine with friends at the posh restaurant on the top floor of the city's tallest building. Half way into the main course, they had a huge barney. For the sake of the other diners, they took their argument out onto the balcony. It is not exactly clear what happened next but a few words like *slag* and *cretin* filtered back into the dining room, where the waiters were lapping up every word. Then there was silence.

Virginia returned to the table alone and enquired whether she had missed dessert. In the end, she could have eaten Rick's soufflé because he wouldn't need it. Somehow, his five foot four frame had fallen over the five foot five balustrade and he had plunged over ninety floors to the pavement below. Of course, there was an investigation and, this time, they disbelieved her story that he had had a bad trip. Everybody knew that Richard O'Flannery didn't do drugs. She was committed for trial and, as an afterthought, the prosecutor decided that it might be a good idea to further investigate the circumstances of Patrick's death.

I know that it will not surprise you to learn that the jury found Virginia Kilpatrick guilty of killing both Pat and Rick and she received two life sentences. The lady maintained that she was acting on holy orders but she really didn't complain all that much. In fact, Ginny found prison life very similar to her time in the convent and she particularly enjoyed the social days with inmates from the men's prison. She even met a lovely chap: an axe murderer called Chopper Mead. Isn't it good to be able to relate to people on a similar level?

FOR YOUR LIES ONLY

Jason was born on the Orient Express during one of those intermittent water stops. Neither Miss Marple nor Hercule Poirot were on board for this particular journey but would have read the birth notices in *The Times*, soon after. Due to the premature nature of the event, the usual qualified medical assistance was not available but the mother was helped through her ordeal by a doctor of divinity, who was traveling in the next compartment. Although the bishop later remarked that the delivery had been as quick and efficient as the Royal Mail, her screams were heard in a number of nearby villages. The residents paid little interest and probably assumed that it was just another murder on the Orient Express.

I have never been able to understand the workings of physic evolution but those who can have stated that childhood experiences are quite often instrumental in formulating life choices. Jason, the 10th Earl of Shropshire, was the first in his family to become an engine driver.

It is not unusual for the Lord of the Manor to assume the mostly ceremonial role as Chairman of the local Historical Society. Over time, his group had restored the abandoned loop line near their rustic railway station and acquired a neat little two-carriage steam train. The track meandered over hill and dale for about ten miles and passed the front gate of Jason's family mansion, Dung Castle. There were three drivers on the roster: Jason, Bert Jones, when he didn't have gout and Sheila Knopplemeyer, the secretary of the Society.

As many of you would know, the upkeep of a castle and the adjoining estate grounds can be quite demanding. Although there was some doubt as to the legitimacy of Jason's entitlement (records indicate that the title was forfeited after the 3rd Earl in 1102 A.D.) there was no doubt about the annual claims for land tax that just kept coming. The family decided that they would open up the house to visitors on weekends and Jason manipulated his roster so that he could train the sightseers in from the main line. His brother, Dilbert, would meet the tourists at the front gate and walk them through the grounds for thirty minutes. Penelope, the unmarried sister, would then take them through the house for a further forty minutes. On completion of the tour, Aunty Mary would provide a lovely Devonshire Tea with double cream scones. All this for twenty-five pounds! It was generally regarded as good value.

During the week, Jason worked for MI6. Yes, he was a spook. Obviously, I can't tell you much about what he actually did but I have it on good authority (from his young children) that he personally knew Burgess, McLean, James Bond and other heroes and villains of Her Majesty's Secret Service. The three kids had vivid imaginations and were always bandying around conspiracy theories, most of which concerned the mysterious husband of Sheila Knopplemeyer. He was from over there and they didn't believe that he really made ice cream for a living. If he had dispatched some of it in their direction, they may well have let him off the hook.

Tom looked directly at Jackson and said "I think he's a German spy. What do you think?" Jackson agreed and they both said it together "Let's get him." Of course, nobody asked Sam but he always agreed with the others, anyway.

I will not delve into the details but the fact that the kids exposed Knopplemeyer and that he did not was a slap in the face for the Earl, who was immediately demoted. The detective work was more Enid Blyton than Vauxhall Cross but those at Secret Service Headquarters needed to save face. They had no option but to eventually give Jason his marching orders.

Fortunately, opportunities opened up at the Historical Society as Sheila Knopplemeyer decided to move out of the area and into a bed-sit near Wormwood Scrubs prison, where her husband would be banged-up for twenty years without remissions. While in prison, he was to write a best-selling book entitled *I Scream*. It became recommended reading for all those who might face incarceration in a British prison.

Although the extra work at the Historical Society filled Jason's time, it didn't fill his pockets and, with a high maintenance wife, three kids and a castle to maintain, unemployment benefits didn't bridge the gap. Of course, he did leave Vauxhall Cross with a part-pension but these people didn't have a sense of humor. His book deal was stymied when he was forced to sign the Official Secrets Act.

I have often said that fate is a lonely hunter and so it was when Jason sat down to a late supper with a visiting American theatrical producer, Russell Sprout, in Soho one evening. Both men were on a downer. Sprout was wallowing in despair after the failure of his West End production and Jason was still unemployed. Jason had redrafted his memoirs to include highly improbable and grossly exaggerated scenarios and he offered a draft copy to Sprout as a possible screenplay.

"Here you go, Russell. It's not exactly West End but Hollywood might like it."

The American was quite enthused by the possibilities of the spy script and showed it to one of his contemporaries, a critically acclaimed showman named Barry Spritzer. So started a successful professional relationship that would last for many years: Spritzer and Sprout.

Spritzer and Sprout were smart and able enough to obtain finance for the film, which had a working title of *Nurse Maybe*. Jason was mortified when he discovered that they had changed the gender of the hero and painted her as a working class girl with questionable morals. Sprout was a realist and correctly surmised that they needed lots of sex to go with the espionage. The Hannah Harlot franchise took off and Spritzer, Sprout and Jason all became quite prosperous on the back of these ground-breaking films. However, this would never be enough for the man from Dung Castle.

Creative people often do their best work when they are poor and I suppose that you could reason that the opposite is also true. Certainly, Jason was now very wealthy and his scripts for the Hannah Harlot movies were terrible, to say the least. Nevertheless, he had slowly acquired an appreciation of the working class, which had been completely foreign to him as an employee of Her Majesty's Secret Service and as a humble Lord of the Manor. He confided to his children that he would never be one of the idle rich and he hoped that they would also embrace similar life aspirations. Little did he know that they were already beyond redemption? He was aware, however, that their mother could never exist without at least three servants and a twice weekly spa treatment. In fact, he included a steam room murder in one of his plots. What a cheeky fellow!

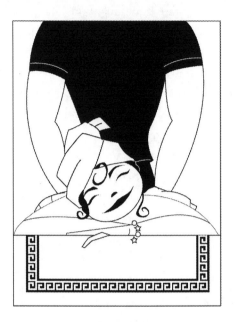

Lady Daphne

Like all writers, Jason craved critical acclamation and so he branched out into other areas of literature. His first completely independent novel focused on a Welsh bank robber who was shot in the foot by the police while trying to escape on a train. It was totally based on the character and persona of Bert Jones, his fellow engine driver with the Historical Society. The man didn't go far for his research.

However, he did go far when family life became too much. The kids had developed into obnoxious, idle toe-rags and his wife had become insufferable. What kind of working conditions were these for a successful author? He didn't tell anyone but went off and purchased a nice little cottage in the Caribbean. The weather was great, the beer was cold and the silence was golden. It was a long way from Dung Castle but the further the better. It was here that he met Maggie, who was also very British. Her cottage was just down the road and she often breezed into town with her young man in tow. Jason never commented on the obvious age difference between the two but made a mental note to consider this as material for his next novel.

The next few years were quite satisfying for Jason. His novels were selling well and he occasionally visited the old country for significant birthdays, marriages and, of course, he had to be there for his own divorce proceedings. It was not an acrimonious parting of the ways as both parties were deliriously happy in their own company. They managed to divvy up the estate without too much interference from their lawyers.

I suspect that some of you may be annoyed that I am half way through my tale and I haven't allocated much time to Jason's spouse but the truth of the matter is that she was an unremarkable woman. Daphne wasn't particularly attractive; she was bourgeois if not boring, a poor mother, highly strung and a hypochondriac to boot. The local pharmacy had her listed as their goldmine client. She popped so many pills every morning and Jason often contemplated slipping in one of those suicide tablets from the Research Department. The trouble is that they were always in the development stage and hardly ever worked.

The last batch was dumped onto the amphetamine market and the pills sold very well as a pick-me-up – not quite what the designers had in mind.

Having said all this, I can understand why you might think that the Jason and Daphne union was a perfect match. The judge didn't think so and granted a decree nisi for the divorce. With this later ratified, Jason returned to his island paradise in high spirits. Maggie put on a bit of a party for the bachelor and the guests that flew in from the old country were all that Jason could have hoped for. I haven't mentioned this before but Margaret had quite a bit of influence at *The Palace*, which was a popular late-night club in central London. Fancy flying in lap dancers for his bachelor party! What a woman.

If there was one drawback to his island living arrangements, it was the fact that our man for all seasons was starting to lose that common touch that he had cultivated in the early days of his literary career. The neighbors were an arty bunch and most of them were independently wealthy. Soirées replaced booze-ups as the favored get-together and celebrities often dropped by. Graeme White, Noel Craven and Howard Bews were regulars.

The first two were also writers and Howard had dabbled in cinema production but could never achieve the same degree of success as Spritzer and Sprout. Craven was different – in fact, very different. His films and plays had been performed on both sides of the Atlantic and he even used to warble a bit, if someone requested a song. Noel may well have been tone deaf but because there was a certain amount of poise to go with the noise, he was enthusiastically accepted. The turn-off for me was the fact that he always used to refer to Jason as *Dear Boy*. The man was already on the wrong side of fifty.

Did I mention that Jason was born on the fourth of July? This was a great talking point for Russel Sprout and he always brought it up when they were in LA for pre-production meetings. For Jason, this was all waffle but it did provide him with some kind of linkage to a way of life that was completely foreign to him.

I think that the expatriate writer might have had a greater impact in America if he had not relinquished his title because the Yanks love all that pomp and ceremony stuff, not that he formally relinquished his birth right – he just didn't use it. It would have been very handy when booking restaurant tables and hotel hookers, not that he did that so often, anymore. For a refined English gentleman, Jason found the West Coast a bit of a cultural desert. If Noel was in town, he would somehow acquire a table at Ciro's or the Brown Derby but Spritzer and Sprout seemed to be happy with Sambo's or Taco Bell. Quite intolerable!

Towards the end of his life, the author often sat in the garden of his tropical retreat and reflected on his career, his transgressions and his conquests. His reflection was mostly transmitted through the bottom of his empty whisky glass but it wouldn't be fair to say that he was a solitary drinker. He often entertained because he needed to liberate all that liquid gold from his wine cellar. The last thing that he wanted was for his kids to get hold of premium booze, especially if it was his. His children had been disappointing and his only fond memory of them was the Knopplemeyer affair, which had been the beginning of the end for him as a servant of the Crown.

Perhaps he should have been more grateful. After all, it is not everybody who can change careers and make the transition so successfully. To the best of his knowledge, his peers in the intelligence community come out of it with a paltry pension and a tap on the shoulder from Her Madge. He certainly didn't need a knighthood – he already had a title that he didn't use.

He went suddenly. A heart attack in the garden of his cottage! Who could ask for a better launching place into the unknown? The cellar was immediately cleared and Maggie, in an inspired tribute to his sense of style, placed a bow-tie around every bottle of Dom Pérignon: to be given to every mourner who attended the funeral. Of course, there were some who insisted on vodka martinis, shaken not stirred but she was over all that. The wake went on for three days, partly due to the late arrival of some of his Irish friends.

Death notices were printed in all the quality newspapers and it was significant that the most heartfelt obituary came from Bert Jones, who was now Chairman of British Rail and the most controversial Welsh person since Black Bart, the pirate. The people at MI6, who sacked him, now lauded him as a hero of the resistance and other Whitehall institutions, such as the Admiralty, the Foreign Office and the Ministry of Defense, also chimed in with various accolades of achievement. For a while, he was getting more print space than Klaus Knopplemeyer, who had just won his fourth Book of the Year award.

You would have to say that his life journey was quite a tale in itself. Jason not only outlasted the Orient Express but also the Dung Castle Express and the mini-cab company that regularly transported him to Boodle's, his private club in London. When he left the country, the cab company went into liquidation.

I think that the world is a better place for having entertained the 10th Earl of Shropshire and there is no doubt that he entertained us. I personally arranged for his notation in *Burke's Peerage*, which is a top-notch publication and it was appropriate that I should also write his epitaph. I think I might now take his story to the masses and may well call my new novel *A Birth on the Orient Express*. I am sure that Agatha Mystery would approve.

'TILL DEATH DO US PART

Roger was in the middle of a messy divorce. However, because one had to think of the children, petulant temper tantrums had to be toned down and confrontations were put on hold when significant occasions occurred: such as Beccy's twenty-first birthday celebration.

Roger wasn't that keen to accept his invitation because he was well aware that his soon-to-be ex-wife had already provided intimate details of his extra marital transgressions to friends and family: her friends and family. His only ally would be his twenty-four year-old secretary, Rachel, who was still an unexposed paramour. What would she think when she discovered all about his other affairs?

"Roger, have you been two-timing me?"

"Only about three or four times, my love!"

After due consideration, he did attend and, as expected, was pretty well socially ignored by one and all. He must have felt like a wet salami sandwich at a vegetarian's barbecue. Given that he had so much time to himself, I think that this is when Roger decided that it would be a good idea to murder Felicity, the mother of his children. He would be left with permanent access to the kids and there would no longer be any alimony to pay. He would also get his home back. People have murdered for less.

Of course, you just don't decide to murder someone. You have to put some thought into it. Certainly, after the dirty deed was done, everybody would know that he was the culprit and he was happy with that; as long as they couldn't prove it. Naturally, there would have to be some finesse attached to the coup de grace and that ruled out the obvious, poisoning. Because Felicity was such a chatterbox, he would have loved to cut her throat but that was also a little bourgeois. He pondered over various options: garroting, hanging, a bullet to the belly and an incendiary device in her powder puff. All of these particular alternatives had merit but I am sorry that he didn't confide in me. I would have suggested that he bore her to death. Then again, I suppose that he had already tried that.

We all have good intentions but you would have to believe that his first homicide attempt could claim little in the way of finesse. I suppose it appeared to be too easy.

Felicity always played cards with the girls on Monday night. Roger was just waiting for Libby's turn to host the evening because she lived on the top of a hill. Yes, he drained the brake fluid from her car. It was as simple as that. The spanner in the works was the fact that it was Georgia's turn to collect the pizza pie and Felicity threw her the keys. The lass in the lime-green Saab hit the pizzeria at over one hundred miles an hour, scattering the take-out queue to all corners of the restaurant. Georgia was thrown from the car and only survived because she landed in a pile of freshly kneaded dough.

Somebody else who would need some dough was Roger. Georgia not only survived but sued the owner of the car for heaps. Our intransient hero had refused to transfer ownership of the vehicle to his wife and so he was liable. Somehow, he concluded that this little episode was the little women's fault and became even more desperate for her to depart this mortal coil.

His spider effort would be regarded as being quite humorous, if it hadn't turned out to be so tragic. I suppose it was easy to get into the house because he still had his key but for the life of me, I don't know where he managed to get hold of a venomous Tarantula. Then he had the bad judgment to drop the critter into his wife's bra drawer. What if Rebecca had wanted to borrow her mom's underwear? On reflection, perhaps this is a bit far-fetched.

What Roger didn't know is that since she had taken up with a bit of a wild stud from her office, Felicity had, all of a sudden, preferred not to wear a bra. One day, she scooped them all up (spider included) and gave the whole collection to the maid.

This is indeed a sad story because the maid was a real perky kind of kid. She always performed her household duties to music and her tastes were quite eclectic. I don't know who found her dead on the floor but when the police arrived, Sting was still playing on her iPod. What were the odds?

I think that Roger came to the conclusion that she was better with animals than he was and so he aborted his plan B, which was to unleash some woman-eating piranha into her bubble bath. He would have had memories of the way Felicity used to demolish those Friday-night fish dinners at the RSL club. Perhaps he felt sorry for the fish.

I don't know how many of you have attempted to murder someone but I would imagine that if you failed twice, you would have to ask yourself whether you are inadequate or just incompetent. Roger wondered if he should bring in another party, a hit-man. He had no idea how to go about it. They don't advertise in the Yellow Pages, do they? He then had a bit of a brainwave, a name from his distant past. I might add; a past that he likes to conveniently forget.

Jugs Malone had a girl-friend called Virginia Slim; who had a pal called Hot Pants Hanrahan. They all used to double date. Jugs had big hands and they had been around a few throats in their time. This was an inspired brainwave.

For fifteen of the last twenty years, Mr Malone's address was reliably steady. You just sent your postal communication to the State's largest penitentiary. As luck would have it, the man with the big hands was currently on parole. He would be delighted to see Roger after all these years. Wouldn't he?

Roger found Jugs in some kind of half-way house but the initial greeting was less than warm. He seemed to vividly remember his first two-year stint in the big house. When he came out, Virginia was no longer slim. She was very pregnant and the finger of suspicion was pointed at Roger. Gulp!

"I promise you, Jugs. That was someone else who was rogering Virginia. Believe me."

In my time, I have met many fast-talking individuals who could sell ice to Eskimos. I think that Roger sits comfortably in the President's chair. I don't know all of what he said to Jugs but, in no time at all, he had him eating out of his hand. They were bosom buddies, once again. All the jail-bird needed was a good honest job that paid well enough to get him back on his feet. Roger definitely had something in mind.

When people meet me for the first time and I tell them that I have never married, the usual retort is "Gee, you must own your own house."

Roger loved his house and when the slag-bag took sole control of his mortgage-free structure, a lot of fond memories went out the door: sunny days in the garden; tinkering in his shed; glorious nights in the doghouse. Jugs could see that he was scarred by the parting experience and was keen to support his mate during hard times. If it meant re-arranging somebody's neck in order to re-establish equilibrium, so be it.

"I'll do it, Roger. Just give me some time to survey the lay of the land." Just because Mr Malone always gets caught, it doesn't mean that he wasn't a professional because he was.

As Jugs didn't know Felicity, it was important to be acquainted with her habits and try and find a window of opportunity in which to strike. After a few days of surveillance, he had isolated her regular haunts: the office, the gym, the hair salon, a trendy wine bar and her favorite restaurant. In fact, he almost chose to impersonate a waiter and give her one last meal, a karate chop. Unfortunately, he would have missed out on his tip so he discounted that one.

Although Roger's name might well be about to be added to the file of infamous cold-blooded murderers, never let it be said that he lacked compassion. He would have no regrets concerning the fate of his former partner but he didn't want any more innocent bystanders to suffer and he advised Malone that there was to be no collateral damage. This instruction didn't go down well. Nevertheless, the hit-man took out his pencil rubber and erased some of his most creative scenarios. The wrecking ball would have been great because he had just renewed his heavy equipment license.

In the end, all this planning came to nothing. Felicity, in fact, did have her last meal at her favorite restaurant. At least, half of it! She choked on a chicken bone in front of two dozen horrified diners and management couldn't do a thing. The Chinese proprietor attended the funeral and advised Roger that they had re-named their signature dish after one of their best customers. *Felicity Fat Wa* was a boneless chicken dish with aromatic spices and a bitter after-taste. It proved to be one of their best take-out performers.

It didn't take long for life to get back to normal. Roger moved back into the family home and the kids resumed their chaotic life. At first, finances became a bit of a problem when Georgia was awarded a large settlement from her legal action but this was offset when Roger sued the Chinese Restaurant over his wife's demise. Swings and roundabouts! Isn't it always the way?

I am sure that there will be more Roger stories at a later date. After all, he is that kind of a guy. Right now, you would never know that he had murder on his mind. He is chairman of the local Arachnophobia Society and has recently become a card player. He has maintained his devotion to the lovely Rachel, who has forgiven him his transgressions and his loyalty even extends to old friends. He employs Jugs Malone as his gardener.

The fellow is very good with lilies and other bereavement flowers.

LAWYERS, NUNS AND MONEY

The other day, I told some folks that I went to Harvard. That was it. There were no probing questions. How long were you there? Was the weather nice? Did you meet any of the students? They just accepted that I went to Harvard.

Because I was wearing a Harvard Law School t-shirt, they may have assumed that I was a lawyer and didn't want to say anything in case the clock was ticking. You know how it is with that lot. Anything that might be construed as billable is usually fair justification. Competition is pretty stiff and work is hard to find. The aggressive marketer is often rewarded. One of my legal friends explained to me that the definition of an optimist is a barrister who has five shirts ironed every week.

Perhaps it is unfair to call some of these people ambulance chasers but I can only relate to my recent DID (drunk in a ditch) experience. It didn't surprise me to see the medics arrive but the attorney was only two minutes behind in his Mercedes. I soon sobered up when I saw his fee structure.

I could go on with a bunch of lawyer jokes but lawyers don't think that they are funny and nobody else thinks they are jokes. Neither am I going to say that lawyers are hard to love but they do seem to be absolutely besotted by their own jurisprudence. Somebody like Geoffrey Robertson QC does have interesting interrogation techniques and his hypotheticals are extremely entertaining. Perry Mason wasn't so bad either.

It has taken me some time to get to the point but much of this narrative is about divorce and so you can't leave out the legal practitioners, can you? Although, I am not an authority on this state of affairs (sic), I have often thought that lawyers are the right people to write the definitive book on matrimony, fine print and all. The last page could be the divorce application.

Please don't assume that all divorce revolves around infidelity. One of the giants of the ad industry has been married six times. He hasn't got time to fool around. I suspect that his wives divorced him because he was just a pain in the ass.

"I am sorry Mrs Simpleton but these circumstances do not provide just cause. That will be $1200. Do you need a receipt?"

Now we come to my school chum, who was a son of a gun. His father was a mobster. Well, we don't call them that in Australia but he was wealthy and Catholic. That gave him an entrée into a very elite education system. He was accepted in the same way as the sons of doctors, lawyers and politicians. In those days, in that school, you could be sanitized from almost anything, except the stigma of divorce. Poor Rodney Razzlefart (not his real name)! They whispered behind his back and demonized his old man, who we all assumed must be promiscuous and a chick magnet. The other lads at boarding school figured that because of this background, Rodney might be able to introduce some of us to a few loose women but this didn't work out. When he finished his studies, he signed up for the priesthood. You can certainly misread people, can't you?

It had always been assumed that Rod would become a lawyer. After all, Big Daddy and all his Mafioso friends were ready-made clients and there was always lots of business there. Rodney didn't seem to have any problem with crime and criminals, which is why I think that he would have made a good lawyer. The only thing that shocks the legal profession is when someone doesn't pay their bill.

What did shock Rodney was his parent's divorce. In recent times, school children have learned to live with this very common state of affairs and can manipulate both parents to their advantage. Rod couldn't imagine his dad with another woman and he didn't want to. He couldn't imagine his mother with any man, his father included. After all, surely she was put on this earth for the sole purpose of loving and nurturing his good self, with the necessary financial assistance from her spouse. This interruption to service was both annoying and unexpected and their trial separation was a time of anguish and distress for him.

Your correspondent wasn't much of a shoulder to cry on as I was busy trying to decide my own future. I wanted to find some way to avoid all that university crap and still end up with a cushy job. The careers officer had lined up an interview with a honey from ASIO, Australia's secret intelligence organization. Somebody had leaked my credentials to ASIO and they were impressed that I was devious, deceitful, sly, cunning and faithless. Contrary to popular belief, intelligence doesn't come into it at all.

This left Father Fanguline as Rod's sole confidante. Fang was his confessor and they got on really well. Rodney used to pass on informed horse-racing tips (from his father) to the priest in the confessional and as a trade-off, received a lighter penance for his transgressions. The cleric offered to pray for a rekindling of the marital harmony and suggested that Rod do the same. He recommended a few saints that would be interested in hearing from him on this issue.

You don't know Rod like I do and I can tell you that this guy never does things by half. He opened his prayer book and systematically trolled the alphabet of saintly piety, which really took quite some time. He started with Saint Andrew, Saint Aloysius and Saint Alimony and continued through the list.

"No, Rod," said the priest. "St Willy is not the patron saint of divorced people."

This was an exercise in futility. By the time that the *decree nisi* was final, Mother had hooked up with a randy chiropodist named Dr Ed Stein, who was a flamboyant character of some notoriety. Mr Razzlefart Senior had now permanently moved out of the family home and was holed up with one of his mistresses.

Rod didn't particularly like Dr Stein and his visits home became more irregular. The influence of his religious mentors became stronger and you are not going to believe this but the youngster actually enjoyed all that praying. For those in the know, it was a slam-dunk that he would enter the seminary.

Seven years later, Rockin' Rod emerged from behind the walls of religious fervor with a round collar and a posting to his first parish, Our Lady of Mount Carmel. I thought that this was quite appropriate as one of his early teenage conquests was a girl named Carmel. Unfortunately, the cute blonde was headed in a different direction: she became an exotic dancer in an inner city nightclub.

We were all there for Rod's ordination. The jam rolls were excellent and he looked relaxed and confident. His mom was proud and looked on with her new husband from the roped off area that was reserved for divorced people. Both of them pretended to be oblivious to the giant fresco of Hades that was hanging in their direct eye-line.

"Look, darling. There's Rodney's friend. Over there in the good seats."

A lot of water can flow under the bridge in seven years and so it was with me. I was getting some occasional work from ASIO but they refused to employ me on a full-time basis due to some personal indiscretions that I don't want to go into. I had been to New Guinea and changed professions. I had become an advertising copywriter and was enjoying the lifestyle. The relaxed hours gave me more time to spend with Rod, who was his own boss for the first time in his life. It goes without saying that he still had to follow certain guidelines that were promulgated by the Pontiff and the Archbishop but there was no problem there; especially as he and the Arch both supported the same football team.

Unfortunately, someone who wasn't at the celebration was Rodney's dear old dad. Two years earlier, he had been gunned down, Chicago style, in one of the city's up-market areas. I wouldn't go so far as to call it a gang war but there were people who had it in for Razzlefart. Surprisingly, the police fingered his brother for the job and the jury agreed. Bart Razzlefart went down for twenty-five years. Rodney just shrugged it off, commenting that they were only half-brothers, anyway.

By the way, did I tell you that his mom married a lawyer? Can you believe that? Not only a lawyer but a mob lawyer! He had a long Italian name that I can't pronounce and always smoked a large cigar. We hit it off and Rod also liked him. In fact, we started a weekly card game in the presbytery of Our Lady's church and, for a while, the prospect of the Sunday collection remaining intact was quite remote.

The fourth member of our group was Willy Wanker. This was not his real name – he thought that we called him that because he owned a chocolate factory. He was, in fact, one of my clients and, without him, the church funds may well have been at risk. He was a terrible card player but liked to think otherwise and was always the first to arrive. If I was any kind of a friend, I would have advised that he spend the night with a good book.

It would have been cheaper. However, you know how it is with advertising people. We have a reputation for always pleasing the client. The following poem, by somebody called anonymous, illustrates that point.

When the client moans and sighs
Make his logo twice the size
When the client's hopping mad
Put his picture in the ad
If he still should prove refractory
Add a picture of his factory.

Willy's factory was churning out a half-decent product and he was always offering Father Rod free samples for his school fêtes and other fund-raising activities; but it was not enough. Our Lady of Mount Carmel was in real financial trouble and the bank was making nasty noises. Rodney's step-father offered to send around someone with an offer that they couldn't refuse. Obviously, a member of the clergy couldn't agree to this kind of a solution and so he prayed to Saint Leo the Lender for divine guidance. It must have worked because I came up with one of my best advertising ideas, yet: to sell some indulgences.

They used to do this in the old days. For three thousand drachmas, you could have your five years in hell reduced to three months in purgatory. We could even do a line for non-Catholics. Willy was delighted with the idea and produced a quality range of chocolates, each box containing an Indulgence Certificate, personally signed by Father Rod Razzlefart, God's servant. There was the Total Indulgence package, the Supreme Indulgence package and the Absolute Indulgence package, which sold for twenty-five thousand dollars and was targeted at politicians, real estate agents and people in the used car business.

Needless to say, the campaign was a great success, although there were a few hiccups. The largest income flow came from Her Majesty's maximum security prison, where there were quite a few wealthy inmates enjoying their custodial sentence. Most of them purchased the premium package and paid in cash. Unfortunately, fifty percent of the takings were found to be counterfeit. I was outraged and wanted to follow up with a Satanic Certificate but Father Rod accepted the shortfall in good grace and intimated that Saint Peter would sort this lot out at the Pearly Gates.

This was the start of it. From then on, he didn't leave me alone. He wanted a sponsor for the girl's netball squad, a logo for the debating team and a media presence for the church choir, which performed at all sacred days plus Hanukkah and Halloween. Some idiot suggested that they dress as pumpkins and I had to arrange that, also.

I may not have mentioned that Our Lady's was adjacent to a Carmelite convent. The nuns fussed over Father Rod like you wouldn't believe. He was still a most attractive man with great charm and generosity of spirit. The Brides of Christ always provided the catering for the weekly poker game and often sat in for a few hands of *Texas hold-em*. I was particularly impressed with Sister Bridget, who always seemed to have an ace up her sleeve and was a far superior player to Willy Wanker. Of course, in the presence of female company, we addressed him as Willy Wonka.

Sister Bridget sits in.

Eventually, Rod got too big for Mount Carmel and was promoted elsewhere in the archdiocese. He became the go-to man wherever there were difficult projects and the media dubbed him *the vicar with a bit of ticker*. He provided informed counsel to the Archbishop and community groups and church administrators.

"Your Grace, this is the best advice I can get from the legal profession. They have waived their usual fee in lieu of an Absolute Indulgence package. I said that you would bless it."

In realty, Father Rod's most trusted advisor was now his step-father. I think that this was because there were so many contentious issues that he had to deal with that could benefit from sound legal thinking and Mario certainly provided that. His experience with Razzlefart Senior had seen him deal with both the Italian and Israeli mobs and he considered himself an expert in both Catholic and Jude Law.

Admittedly, there were a number of disagreements with Mario and Bishop Anderson, who was Rod's immediate superior. These were mostly disputes over the best way to cut one's losses: through legal means or public relations. I don't have to tell you that the Catholic Church was under worldwide pressure for any number of indiscretions committed in their name and the pressure on the purse strings was immense. They sold artwork and properties and even trebled the naming-right fees for their sporting affiliations, in particular, the Cardinals. In Arizona and Missouri, representatives of these teams cried foul.

Irrespective of these disagreements, Mario and the support that he provided was appreciated and his demise was a great shock to everyone. Although he had many friends, he must also have had enemies. Somebody had slipped a poisonous snake into his linguine and he had consumed it with a glass of award-winning Chianti that he kept in his substantial cellar. Rod rushed home to console his mother, who immediately came under suspicion because they finished the bottle before calling the police.

Surprisingly, the exit of Mario from the cathedral think-tank proved a turning point in Rod's life. The bishop felt that his legacy could be maintained if Rod himself were to take on legal studies and gave him sabbatical leave to study at Harvard. What a turn-around! Didn't I tell you that it was always expected that he would end up as a lawyer? He is now a resident of Boston and he has almost completed his course. In fact, I visited him this year and he remains as generous as ever. He gave me a t-shirt.

THE PITTS AND THE PENDULUM

The other night, I had the most unbelievable experience. Angelina Jolie was sitting on my knee, completely naked. She was holding a single red rose and singing a song that my grand-father would remember well: "If I was the only girl in the world and you were the only boy."

Yes, of course it was a bloody dream. Everybody knows that Angie can't sing.

Ahhh, the stuff of dreams! Where does one acquire the fodder to nourish these scenarios of slumber? Certainly, if you already have a vivid imagination, you can get the engine ticking over but there is always a need for a bit of a heart starter and I categorically blame my doctor for my night time excursions. His waiting room has the greatest collection of trashy magazines that I have ever laid eyes on. Every move that Angelina has made over these past few years has been recorded for posterity and, although many will say that you are a sick person to be even remotely interested, I will say that is why I am in my GP's waiting room. I am a sick person.

I want you to know that all of my dreams don't have a sexual connotation – only about ninety percent of them. I can remember when I was a playing a gig with Dolly Parton and the Dixie Chicks in a Nashville bath-house. To this day, I don't know why the electric guitars didn't fuse in the hot tub. Many of us are chased in our dreams and I can relate to that because of the work that I do.

"Tell me, doctor. I am continually being chased. Is this a dream or a nightmare?"

"It depends on whether your pursuer is male or female. That will be $600. Do you have Medicare?"

I don't know why I decided to see an analyst but you have to admit that it is a very American thing to do. I never thought that a clear-thinking, god-fearing, hard-drinking sex-maniac would share his thoughts and passions with anyone other than his best friend or cell-mate. Then, along came a person with a fancy name and a couch. They offered to mend relationships and interpret dreams. Now, I ask you, where would they learn something like that?

If I hadn't have been an avid viewer of that superb television series, *The Sopranos*, I would have definitely had doubts about a female psychiatrist. The first session was all right but I became increasingly nervous thereafter. Should I tell her that she was now the one who was sitting naked on my knee? Of course, it would never have come to this if she had decent reading material in her waiting room.

Tony Soprano never got around to having his psychoanalyst whacked. I can understand that he might have considered it because they do ask the most personal questions. This would be understandable if they were happy with your answers but they never are. They proceed to try and wheedle out even more intimate details from your closet of clandestine secrets. And what about those tape recorders? Tell me that they don't replay them at their annual *Nutter of the Year* dinner dance.

The Dream of Olwen was a classic piano piece from a 1947 movie entitled *While I live*. Olwen really didn't take much part in the movie because all the action takes place twenty-five years after her death. However, that didn't stop all the contemporary pianists of the time from jumping on the bandwagon and that included Mantovani and Liberace. It was also a party piece for people who had two names. I am not sure which version my therapist used on me but she did explain that music was a great relaxant and that I should consider it as a substitute for marijuana and amphetamines. Can you believe that I was paying for this advice?

When Edgar Allan Poe wrote *The Pit and the Pendulum*, it was not so much a bad dream but a horror story. Is there anything worse than falling into a bottomless pit? My shrink told me that dreams about falling are very common and tend to indicate insecurity and anxiety. Although this information was absolutely riveting, I didn't care. I mostly have dreams about sex. Does that make me a bad person?

I realize that I am not the only person to have had a dream. Certainly, my efforts pale in comparison to those of Martin Luther King and Mary Shelley, who dreamt up Frankenstein. Paul McCartney wrote *Yesterday* on the back of a sleepless night and other songwriters have brought their dreams into reality: from Stephen Foster to Bobby Darin and Andrew Lloyd Webber.

Am I a beautiful dreamer, a dream lover or will any dream do? I suspect that this whole thing is one-way traffic but should Angelina once more wish to come to the party, she knows where it is – same time, same place. Turn off the light, will you, Jennifer?

THE FINAL JOURNEY

The other evening, I watched a Fox Classic Movie. It was an adaption of Herman Melville's best-selling novel, Moby Dick. For the life of me, I can't imagine why anybody would name a whale *Dick*. You probably know the tale of the eccentric, one-legged Captain Ahab (as mad as a cut snake) and his pursuit of the monster mammal, which had been responsible for the loss of his limb. He chased the pile of blubber across hell and high water with no regard for his own safety or the safety of his crew.

Like many of his contemporaries, Ahab was a Quaker but you wouldn't want to sit across the breakfast table from him. He was sour, dour and socially inadequate but he did have the smarts as far as the big fish were concerned. Did you know that without devices like our modern sat-nav, he plotted, in great detail, the seasonal travels of the gigantic white bull whale? The big fella covered a lot of territory and quickly – just like Japanese tourists on a shopping excursion.

Most of my reference material concerning water-borne activities comes from my good friend Richard Head, whose family still holds their long-term license for the naval latrine. Richard maintains that if you pet whales instead of harpooning them, they will roll over and do tricks. I think that Captain Ahab may have rubbed his whale the wrong way because the brute dumped on his ship and sent it and most of his Nantucket crew to Davy Jones' locker.

I am truly sorry for spoiling the end of the movie for you. I can be a real Jonah at times.

I hope that you are not bored with my little sea shanty because sometimes I can bore people to distraction. There are so many important issues out there and yet I am ruminating on my television viewing. The thing is that I am getting old and when you get old, death does become a distraction. You often wonder what lies ahead.

The other day I received a coupon with my copy of *Seniors News*.

It was from a cryogenic company and they offered me a no-obligation preservation and restoration package. Richard knows all about this and he filled me in. They are a holding company with refrigeration facilities. They freeze your body and store it away in a warehouse. When someone eventually discovers a fountain-of-youth potion, which is bound to happen, they will restore you back to life. You can then be anyone or anything you want to be: a Riviera playboy, David Beckham or Kylie Minogue's ass. It all sounded pretty good to me.

You can choose budget or premium packages and this does not so much depend on where they put you but who they put you with. I believe that Pamela Anderson has already signed up and as I expect that she will go before I do, that means that I will end up on top of her. This has been a lifelong ambition of mine.

In truth, I will probably only be able to afford the budget package, which gives you cremation. They were a bit vague about the restoration bit but it had distinct advantages. Limited storage space is required and they lend you out to your family for Christmas and Thanksgiving. I can be popped into the kitchen freezer while the rest of the relatives are tucking into the turkey. "Here's to Uncle Gerry." Just be sure that you thoroughly check out the sprinkling when they serve the ice cream.

When the time comes for me to cross over to the other side, I suspect that I will want to take my golf clubs with me – not to gain any perceived advantage when I play the Paradise Waters layout but as a charitable act in relation to the person who might otherwise inherit the clubs. This sporting equipment is defective. I can never hit a good score.

In heaven, they always match you up with players of similar standard and I think that it is pertinent to say that I am the kind of bloke who would never begrudge a fellow competitor his chance at a mulligan, should he or she stuff-up their first shot. I am not so tolerant about awarding a finnegan, which happens when your second shot is even worse than your first. Even away from the golf-course, I know that I am going to meet a lot of Irish friends in paradise including O'Connell, O'Keefe, O'Rourke and O. Henry. I like to rubber nose with celebrities, especially sports people and I can't wait to reminisce with Bradman and Babe Ruth and take a Sunday drive with Fangio or Ayrton Senna.

If there is one doubt that I have about this final journey, it is the possible reunion with people that I don't really care about. Let's face it. What will Captain Ahab have to say to Moby Dick? For Lizzie Borden, who chopped up her folks with an axe in Massachusetts, there is sure to be an awkward silence. "Sorry Mom. Sorry Pop."

Having said this, I do realize that there are geographical divisions in the great big palace in the sky and I can recall from my religious instruction that the basement area is called Hades. This place is reserved for murderers, pedophiles and tabloid journalists. I must remember to visit my last editor. I am sure that is where he will be.

When I go, I hope that I go quickly. When you hang around for too long with a terminal illness, bookmakers get involved. This is certainly the case with the crowd that I mix with. They will bet on anything and the bag men have to take into consideration the long-term effects of their business if I am no longer around to fund their lifestyle. If this cryogenic thing doesn't work out, I may opt for a termination at sea followed by a Viking's funeral – I saw this in a film once and it looked fantastic.

The Sea Shall Not Have Them was the name of a gritty British movie that was produced in the fifties. Quite frankly, it can have me. Surely the sharks can't be as bad as some of the people I have met on terra firma. With the price of a cemetery plot, these days, a watery grave can cut out a lot of middle men.

Some of my friends disappeared into the briny in the traditional Italian way but I think that this might be a little too sudden. When you are wearing concrete boots, you tend to sink so fast that you miss most of the scenery on the way down. Nevertheless, I think that this is the way that my friend, Paddy Pest, might go. They have already tried to poison his pasta and this would be the logical step thereafter. Paddy probably feels that he has already been to hell and back but I think that he is deluding himself if he thinks that he is going to get out of there. Once they sight his CV, he will be their hottest recruit since Errol Flynn and Ted Bundy.

I hope you don't mind me rambling on about death like this. They say that confrontation is good for the soul and that it is best to face your demons before you actually meet them. Lucifer loves you. It is as simple as that. After the intense inferno of a Viking's funeral, the complimentary chili dog that you receive on arrival will seem like a cooling balm. Then there are all his real cool friends.

"Hello, my name is Jack the Ripper. Have you met Billy the Kid and Vlad the Impaler?"

I'm talking real color, here. These are no bible-bashing do-gooders with a propensity to forgive and forget. These are the dregs of society and all of them have stories to tell that will rock your socks. Bring it on, baby.

This brings me back to Nantucket. I was there last year but I think that I would like to return one last time. Perhaps, if I could get together a motley crew, we might dance across the white waves and have a whale of a time. For those of you who are land-lubbers, there will be a small corner of a field somewhere: a place where you can reflect on the wild oats that you have sown and the intensity of your depravity. The Grim Reaper will eventually roll in with the west wind and you must give him his due. It is inevitable. See you in hell.

The End

GERRY BURKE

ABOUT THE AUTHOR

Gerry Burke has now written three books that highlight the humorous aspects of politics, entertainment, sport and travel. His home base is Melbourne, Australia, where he has taken early retirement from his previous employment as a copywriter and Creative Director.

The author has traveled extensively and boasts a wealth of life experience, which has been mostly usurped by his alter ego, Paddy Pest. For their sins, the Catholic Church and the Irish nation are frequent victims of his witty revelations.

Gerry's father came to Australia with a degree in blarney and promptly enrolled his only son in a Jesuit school. The revelations in this book have been a long time coming.

Other books by Gerry Burke:

From Beer to Paternity – one man's journey through life as we know it
Down-Under Shorts – stories to read while they're fumigating your pants

Printed in the United States
By Bookmasters